Romance Unbound Publishing

Presents

The Inner Room

Claire Thompson

Edited by Donna Fisk
Jae Ashley

Cover Art by Kelly Shorten
Fine Line Edit by Kathy Kozakewich

Print ISBN 978-1499787139
Copyright 2014, Claire Thompson
All Rights Reserved

Chapter 1

The naked woman in the video was on her hands and knees, a bucket of sudsy water beside her, a large sponge in her hand. Marissa sucked in her breath as she watched Master Mark lift his heavy black boot and bring it to rest on the woman's back. The woman's face was obscured by her long blond hair. Marissa could sense the sudden tension in the woman's body, though she continued to move her hand in wide circles over the stone floor. Master Mark pressed down with his boot until the woman collapsed onto her stomach on the cold, wet floor.

"Why are you here, slave L?" Master Mark asked in his deep, sexy British accent. He moved his boot along her back until it rested on the nape of her neck.

The camera moved in for a close-up of slave L's face, capturing what seemed to be genuine fear in her wide blue eyes. "Because I was a dirty little slut, Sir," she replied in a tremulous voice.

Master Mark laughed. "We already know that, slave. What precisely did you do that resulted in this particular punishment?" He slid his boot to her cheek and then lifted it, leaving a wet streak of dirt behind. Crouching beside her, he tucked strands of blond hair behind her ear and Marissa was struck by the tender expression now on Master Mark's face.

"I was touching myself without permission, Sir," the girl whispered.

Marissa sighed and shifted on the bed. She slipped her hand between her legs, her fingers seeking her throbbing clit. Though intellectually she was repelled by the man's treatment, emotionally she thrilled to it. Defenses lowered by her arousal, Marissa had to admit in her heart of hearts she yearned to be that naked girl lying on the wet stone waiting for her stern master's retribution.

Master Mark wrapped his hand in slave L's thick hair and twisted it back from her scalp. She winced but remained otherwise still. "That's correct," Master Mark said. "You touched my property without my express permission. Get up." He tugged her hair to pull her upward.

As the woman struggled to her feet, he continued, "Time for part two of your punishment. Stand at attention, hands locked behind your head, legs shoulder-width apart." The camera pulled back, revealing the long, whippy cane Master Mark now held in his hand. "Twenty strokes," he intoned. "You will maintain your position, and you will thank me for each stroke."

The slave cast a fearful glance at the cane. "Yes, Sir," she breathed. Marissa could see the tremble in her limbs and the faint sheen of sweat on her face. Master Mark's cock bulged in his leather pants. If these were actors, they were doing a hell of a job.

The camera angle shifted again, giving Marissa a good view of the woman's back, ass and long legs that ended in very high, shiny black heels. The cane hissed in the air. Marissa winced as it struck the backs of the woman's thighs. "Thank you!" the woman yelped.

Marissa rubbed herself with fingers lubricated by her desire as Master Mark struck the woman over and over, leaving red, angry stripes on her thighs and ass. When the camera moved to her face, it was twisted in an expression that could have been agony or ecstasy.

"Oh, thank you, Sir. Thank you! Oh!" slave L cried.

Marissa's mouth was dry, her breath a rasp in her throat, her fingers flying in the wet heat between her legs as the Master with the hard eyes and cruel smile struck the willing masochist on the screen again and again. A warm tingling sensation rose deep in Marissa's belly, culminating in a shivery burst of sensation as her cunt spasmed in release.

Her hand fell away and she closed her eyes with a sigh. She lay limp, no longer focused on the scene still playing on her laptop screen. When she could rouse herself sufficiently from her orgasm-induced lethargy, she reached for the laptop, where slave L was now on her knees slurping and sucking Master Mark's huge cock with enthusiastic abandon.

Marissa clicked away from the site and closed down the laptop. Her immediate urges satisfied, the usual vague feelings of shame and dissatisfaction began to reemerge in her psyche. Why was she like this? She was a medical doctor, a professional who had always held her own in her romantic relationships. What was wrong with her that she got off watching women be degraded and sexually tortured? Even worse, why did she long with such a deep and abiding intensity to *be* one of those women?

Oh, get over yourself. Marissa could almost hear her friend Dana's voice in her head. *It's a consensual act. They both like and want what's happening. Stop beating yourself up for your feelings.* If only she could be more like Dana, who was completely comfortable in her own skin and fully accepting of her masochistic tendencies and sexual needs.

Maybe if I found the right guy, Marissa thought, not for the first time. *Someone who would just know what I want without my having to spell it out.* She snorted at this line of thinking. If there was a Prince Charming, or rather a Master Charming, out there somewhere waiting to sweep her off her feet, he sure was taking his sweet ass time about it. Or maybe he just couldn't find his way to the hospital where she spent most of her waking hours.

Pushing these unproductive thoughts from her mind, Marissa reached for her smart phone and set the alarm for five a.m. That should give her time to get to the gym for her workout before hospital rounds at seven. She reached for the lamp and turned it off. Pulling the covers to her chin, she closed her eyes.

~*~

"Hey, Dana, I didn't see you out there this morning." Marissa reached for a second towel and wound it around her head. Her workout had been good, and she'd already decided she would permit herself a muffin later that morning.

Dana, who had been coming to the same Manhattan health club for the three years Marissa had been a member, stepped from the shower stall beside Marissa's. They had become friends, and they met for lunch whenever their busy schedules permitted. Though they only managed to get together a few times a month, Marissa had found herself opening up to Dana in a way she rarely had with anyone else.

"Oh, hey there, girlfriend," Dana replied. "Yeah, I got here early so I could soak in the hot tub after my workout. How're you doing?"

"I'm good," Marissa said automatically. "How are you?"

"Great," Dana said with way too much enthusiasm for six in the morning. She turned away to reach for her towel and Marissa's heart did a little flip in her chest.

Dana's ass and the backs of her thighs were striped with brownish-red welts. Dana glanced back. "What are you looking at?" She followed Marissa's gaze and shrugged. "Oh, that. We had a totally hot session last night. Tony got a little, uh, overenthusiastic. I loved it."

Dana had always been open with Marissa about her lifestyle, as she called it. In fact, once Marissa had finally gotten up the nerve to admit she was curious, Dana was the one who had turned her on to the BDSM training sites that now provided the secret fodder for Marissa's late night masturbatory activities. Dana was unapologetically submissive and masochistic, and claimed she was "owned" by her husband, Tony, a concept that at once baffled and deeply intrigued Marissa.

"Are those cane marks?" Marissa whispered, though the other women in the locker room were busy dressing, blow-drying their hair and applying makeup. No one was paying them the slightest bit of attention.

Dana grinned proudly and nodded as she reached back with one hand to touch her welted thigh. "I earned each stroke, thank you, and the orgasm Tony gave me afterward would have blown my socks off, if I'd been wearing any."

Marissa felt suddenly hot. The skin on her own thighs and ass actually tingled with sympathetic longing. What would it be like to experience the sharp cut of a cane, the stroke a whip, the feel of a heavy boot pressed against her cheek?

To distract herself as much as anything from the turmoil raging in her brain, Marissa said, "Come over here. Let me examine your skin."

"Yes, Dr. Roberts." Dana gave her a mock salute, but she moved obediently to stand with her back to Marissa, who was seated on the bench between the lockers. Marissa gingerly touched the skin on Dana's thigh, which was welted but not broken. She could feel the slight heat radiating from the affected areas as Dana's skin rallied to heal itself.

"What do you use to care for the wounds?" Marissa asked.

"They're not wounds," Dana retorted, flopping down to sit beside Marissa. "They're marks of courage and honor, and I cherish them." The flippancy was gone from her tone. "But to answer your question, we treat my marks and bruises with arnica cream. It's part of Tony's aftercare ritual."

"Aftercare?" Marissa was always fascinated by the glimpses Dana gave her of their lifestyle, and, if she were honest, not a little jealous. The way Dana talked about BDSM made it sound like the most romantic thing on the planet, which confused Marissa, but intrigued her nonetheless.

Dana pulled on her thigh-high stockings as she spoke, reminding Marissa she needed to get ready as well. She rose from the bench and busied herself in front of the mirror, but she was all ears.

"Well," Dana said, moving to stand beside Marissa, her makeup bag in hand. "After the intensity of a play session, Tony rewards me for what he calls the gift of my submission." She smiled dreamily. "A scene can really take it out of you. It's not just about the physical thing—the whipping or bondage or what have you." Just these words sent a shiver through Marissa, and she marveled as she always did at

Dana's ease and comfort in tossing around what for Marissa were highly charged words. "Submission can also take a huge emotional toll. When you do it right, you give of your whole self — it's a complete exchange of power, and it can be incredibly intense, and, frankly, exhausting. Sometimes I can't even move for, like, ten minutes. I mean, I'm conscious and everything, but I'm off floating somewhere, and I lose the capacity to think or use my muscles or anything. Other times I might burst into tears."

"Tears?" Marissa echoed, looking at Dana in the mirror.

Dana shrugged. "Not sad tears. It's more of a release. Tony will just hold me and whisper sweet things in my ear. He tells me to take my time and come back to earth when I'm ready. He'll do stuff like put the arnica cream on my skin, or wash my body with a warm washcloth, or give me a massage. I love the aftercare almost as much as I love the play, if you want to know the truth. Everyone loves to be touched, but it's more than that. Tony makes me feel cherished and adored."

Marissa busied herself with her makeup, trying to recall the last time a man had held her in his arms, a man who made her feel cherished and adored. *Let's see,* she mused as she applied her lipstick, *I guess that would have been...never.*

~*~

Cam cursed softly under his breath. *Not again*, he thought. His aide, Becky, had just called in at the last minute to say she was sick and wouldn't be coming in. It was the third time in the ten days he'd been in the new job that she'd done that, and always at the last second. Cam knew the aides were paid next to nothing, and he also knew you got what you paid for. In every hospital he'd ever worked in there was always a problem with aides not showing up or leaving mid-shift or just not doing a good job. As a registered nurse, Cam's plate was more than filled with direct patient care duties and supervising his healthcare team. While he hated to complain, he flat out didn't have time to change bedpans and fluff pillows.

Cam finished the chart he was working on and glanced at his watch. If he worked quickly, he'd manage at least to make sure his patients were clean and comfortable, and maybe he could get another aide to cover by the afternoon. Armed with a pile of fresh linens, Cam began to move down the corridor. As he walked past Mrs. Watson's room, he heard a soft moan of pain and stopped short.

Mrs. Watson had just arrived the day before, brought in by a concerned neighbor who found her lying on the floor of her bathroom, where she'd taken a tumble while stepping out of her tub. Fortunately, the only immediate thing wrong with her was a broken wrist—a broken hip would have been far more serious. But beyond the fracture, Mrs. Watson was elderly, frail and clearly disoriented. She was malnourished and probably barely eking out an existence on her social security check. She had no family to speak of, and, Cam suspected, suffered as much from loneliness as anything. Cam had made a request for social services, but meanwhile he hoped to make Mrs. Watson as comfortable as possible for as long as Medicare allowed her to be in the hospital.

He stopped at her open door and knocked lightly. "Good morning, Mrs. Watson. May I come in?"

There was no response. Cam stepped into the room. Though her eyes were closed, the old woman's mouth was twisted into a rictus of pain, one gnarled hand clenching the sheet.

"Mrs. Watson?" Cam said gently, moving closer. "Can I make you more comfortable?"

She moaned again. She didn't move or open her eyes. Cam lowered the guardrail and sat carefully on the edge of the bed. "Mrs. Watson? Emily?"

At the sound of her first name, her grimace relaxed, if just a little. Cam reached for her hand in an effort to ease her death grip on the sheets. Like a child, she curled her cold, dry fingers around his index finger and sighed softly, though she still didn't open her eyes.

"Emily," Cam said again, "can I get you something? Some water? A fresh pillow?"

Mrs. Watson rolled her head in his direction, wisps of white hair barely covering her pink scalp. "George," she croaked in a tiny voice, her eyes still closed. "George, I knew you would come." She squeezed tighter on Cam's finger.

"Yes, Emily," Cam said softly, his heart aching for the lonely old woman. "I'm here now. You can let go of the pain. You can sleep."

Her grip loosened on his finger and she sighed, her face slackening, her breathing deepening. Cam sat there a full minute longer, until he was sure she was resting comfortably. Carefully he eased his hand from hers. Raising the guardrail, he slipped quietly from the room.

~*~

Marissa surreptitiously watched the new nurse as he leaned over a chart in the nurses' station. His hair was a little long, curling around his ears and on the back of his neck, though it was neatly brushed back from his face. It was rich chestnut brown, and Marissa had a sudden fantasy of running her fingers through the thick, shiny locks. He wore dark blue scrubs over broad shoulders and muscular arms. Probably in his late twenties, he had a good face, she thought, with strong bones, sparkling, kind blue eyes and a ready smile.

All the nurses and aides had been buzzing about "the new guy" since he'd arrived on the floor. A male nurse was still unusual enough for comment, but a seriously good-looking one was enough to set them all in a tizzy. "Probably gay," Lawanda, Marissa's favorite nurse on the unit, had informed Marissa on Cam's first day. "A guy that hot, that in shape, and a nurse? Got to be gay."

Marissa wasn't so sure, but firmly told herself it didn't matter in the least what the man's sexual orientation was, or anything else about him, as long as he did his job. She even told herself she was mildly annoyed he'd been assigned to her floor, since his presence distracted the staff, though they'd get used to him soon enough.

Marissa's phone buzzed and she reached into her lab coat to glance at it. It was a text message from Dana. *Girlfriend, exciting news! Call me when you get a chance, k?*

Marissa ducked into her office to make the call. When she opened her office door, she was disconcerted to see someone at her desk. Phil Mitchell looked up with a smarmy smile.

"What are you doing in my office?" Marissa demanded. "That's my personal laptop. What do you think you're doing?" She advanced quickly into the room. She distinctly remembered leaving her laptop on the credenza behind the desk, but now it was on the desk in front of Phil, his hand resting on top of it.

He lifted his hands as if in surrender. "Relax, I thought it was one of the hospital-issued laptops, but I realized my error right away." He flashed a boyish grin at her. "Fear not, lovely lady. All your secrets are safe with me."

Marissa frowned, angry with Phil for his presumption and overfriendly manner, especially after the debacle at that happy hour. She could feel the heat in her face and knew she was blushing, which just made her madder. Why had Nancy let this guy waltz in there like he owned the place? She folded her arms across her chest. "I'm sorry—what were you doing again in here? Does the secretary know you're in here?"

"Not to worry. I'm cleared through the tech department to install the latest upgrade on all physician and nursing station PCs. I'm just finishing up here, and then I'll be out of your hair." Swiveling toward her office computer keyboard, he tapped a few keys and pushed away from her desk. "That should do it. You're all set."

He moved past her in the small office, his arm brushing her shoulder. The unwelcome contact sent a shiver down her spine. Turning back at the door, Phil moved his eyes insolently from her face to her body and then back again. "Let me know if you have any problems. Any problems at all, Doc."

"I'll be sure to do that," Marissa said firmly. *Over my dead body.*

She closed the door and moved toward her chair. Marissa would have to talk to Nancy about letting unaccompanied people into her office. The idea of

Phil Mitchell being in her private space sent an unpleasant shudder of distaste through her.

She sank down into her chair, her mind whirling back over the disastrous happy hour the week before. The IT company the hospital was using had arranged a "meet and greet" for medical and administrative staff most affected by the software changes. They had reserved a room at a nearby restaurant and had provided hors d'oeuvres and an open bar.

Marissa had decided to attend, part of a promise to herself to be more social at hospital events. She'd barely eaten over the course of the day and made the mistake of having two Bay Breeze cocktails in a row, which slid down way too easily and then went straight to her head. When Phil Mitchell had appeared beside her at the bar with his blond good looks and ready smile, she'd been friendlier than she might have been without the lubricant of alcohol.

He was maybe a little too full of himself, but what the hell, he was young, single and seemingly captivated by her. She could admit now in retrospect, she'd been flattered by his attention and apparent interest.

Still, she had been stunned by his move when she came out of the women's restroom toward the end of the event. The restrooms were located at the back of the restaurant in a darkened alcove. Without a word, he'd slammed her against the wall, pressed his mouth against hers and tried to force his tongue between her lips while grinding his erection against her body.

She'd shoved him hard, sending him sprawling backward. "What the hell do you think you're doing!" she'd demanded, breathless with shock.

He'd looked confused for a second as he righted himself. Then a flash of pure, venomous rage had flickered over his features before being extinguished by a conciliatory smile. "Hey, come on, baby. What gives? The way you were flirting with me back at the bar, I thought—"

"You thought wrong," she'd snapped, still taken aback by the guy's nerve.

"Hey, Doc, no hard feelings. Just crossed wires, huh?"

Embarrassed by the whole situation, Marissa nodded. "Okay. Yeah, whatever."

She was still angry, not only him, but at herself for letting liquor momentarily affect her better judgment, and had decided it was time to leave. While saying her goodbyes to Fred Hession and the other top brass, she had felt Phil's eyes on her. She'd glanced toward him, disconcerted by his cold, hard stare. Marissa had shuddered, glad she hadn't made the horrible mistake of actually going out with such a creep.

She'd managed to avoid him over the past week while he worked all the bugs out of the hospital's computer systems. As he moved around the unit, he flirted shamelessly with the female staff, and most of them seemed to eat it up, giggling and batting their eyelashes at the handsome young computer technician. He hadn't apologized to Marissa for his behavior, and she'd told herself it was just as well — she would put the whole sorry event behind her. It was over and done with, and soon, thank god, he'd be gone.

Marissa got paged almost as soon as she'd shooed the unwelcome Phil out of her office. It was nearly five o'clock before she had a chance to respond to Dana's text. Flopping into her desk chair, she tapped a message onto the screen. *Hey, Dana. Crazy day. What's up?*

A moment later her phone buzzed with an incoming call from Dana. Swiveling in her chair to face the tiny window of her cramped office that looked out over the vista of the Manhattan skyline, Marissa took the call. "Hi," she said, trying and not quite succeeding to censor the image of Dana's naked, welted body from her mind. "What's up?"

"Open invitation night, that's what," Dana said cryptically.

When she didn't elaborate, Marissa said, "Okay, I'll bite. What's open invitation night? Are you inviting me over to watch Master Tony in action?" As soon as the words tumbled from her mouth, she wished she could grab them back. She'd only been kidding as she said it, but what if that was what Dana was offering? Did she dare accept? Would they expect her to participate? Did she want to?

Dana laughed. "Even better. You know that BDSM club we belong to? Once a month we're allowed to bring guests and prospective members to see what the place is about. Tony asked me if I'd like to bring you and—"

"Tony knows about me?" Marissa blurted, not quite sure how she felt about that.

"Sure. I tell Master Tony everything, you know that. He's always interested in anyone who's curious about the scene. He's got this personal mission to bring BDSM to the world." She laughed and continued, "He's suggested before that I bring you around, but I was pretty sure you weren't ready. Then after I saw the way you were looking at me this morning, your tongue practically hanging out, your eyes so full of longing I thought you were going to cry—"

"What?" Marissa exploded, embarrassed she'd been so transparent. "I never did any such thing."

Dana's voice was kind. "Hey, Marissa, honey. I'm sorry if I'm pushing buttons. I do tend to just blurt things out, you know. Master Tony says that's what gags are for." Again she laughed. "Anyway, seriously, can you honestly tell me you weren't, if not turned on, at least intrigued about those cane marks?"

When Marissa didn't respond, Dana went on, "You're thirty-two years old, right? In the three years

I've known you, I've watched you date the occasional guy and lose interest in like five minutes, no matter how nice or good-looking or rich or hung or whatever the dude might be. You've talked before about wishing you could find a guy you connected with, but that it's virtually impossible to meet anyone, given your schedule and the dwindling supply of decent single guys in the city."

"Yeah," Marissa admitted, though she knew the issue went deeper than mere availability of single men. Several times over the course of the day, Marissa had found herself falling into a daydream in which *she* was the cherished and adored sub girl, lying in the arms of her Dom after an especially intense play session, as Dana called them. She didn't just want any available guy in the right socio-economic bracket. She wanted what Dana had.

Dana continued, unwittingly giving voice to Marissa's thoughts. "Every time I talk about the scene, or you witness the latest evidence of Tony's and my delicious games, you look like a kid with her face pressed up against the glass of a candy store. Yet, as far as I know, and please correct me if I'm wrong, the only thing you've done to find out if the lifestyle is for you is masturbate to BDSM porn videos, am I right?"

Marissa's ears felt hot, and she was glad this was a phone conversation, instead of face to face, as she knew she was blushing. "Oh, I, um," she stammered, though Dana had in fact hit the nail on the head.

"Want to know what I think?" Dana continued, thankfully not pressing Marissa for a more coherent response. "I think you're just not looking in the right place. I think it's time for you to take the bull by the horns. Stop acting like a little girl and find the courage to explore your true feelings and desires. The Power Exchange is opening its outer room to guests tonight, and I'm inviting you."

Dana had mentioned The Power Exchange before—a private BDSM venue for folks who were seriously into the BDSM lifestyle. Dana and Tony engaged in what Dana called public scenes, which Marissa surmised from Dana's occasional descriptions included whips, chains, rope, gags and lots of naked bodies. Marissa imagined something out of a gothic horror film—whipping posts, torture racks, manacles protruding from crumbling stone walls, everything cast in a blood-red light, the only sound that of cracking leather and anguished cries.

Marissa felt the heat rising in her crotch. Her breasts ached and she reached her free hand into the cup of her bra to tweak the suddenly distended nipple. She shifted in her chair and pressed her thighs together in an effort to ease the ache in her sex, glad her office door was closed.

"Marissa? You there?"

"Yeah," Marissa said hoarsely. She cleared her throat. "Yes, I'm here."

"So, how about it? You ready to stop being the kid with her nose pressed to the glass and step on inside? Shall we come by your building at nine o'clock to pick you up?"

Dana was right. Marissa's excuses all her life about why she had no time for a relationship were pretty worn at this point. She was done with medical school. She was done with residency. She had a good staff position at a well-respected city hospital. She understood intellectually there was nothing wrong with being a sexual masochist. Was she ready, at last, to finally begin her own erotic exploration into BDSM?

Marissa was silent for a long moment. She felt as if she were poised on the edge of a high dive. Closing her eyes, she took the leap. "Yes, nine o'clock sounds good."

"That a girl," Dana said approvingly.

Marissa felt almost giddy with excitement, but she managed to keep her tone calm as she asked, "So, what do I wear to this place?"

"Doesn't matter. You'll have to strip at the door anyway."

There was a beat of silence while Marissa struggled to process this latest information. "Wait, what?" she finally managed. "Are you serious?"

Dana laughed. "Just kidding, silly. You can wear jeans, a dress, whatever you want. But I should warn you, there will be some folks there who are naked, or nearly so. I figure you can handle that, being a doctor and all."

Marissa thought about this and decided that yes, she could handle it. "What about you? What're you wearing?"

"Whatever Master Tony lays out for me. Probably something short, tight and low cut. He likes to show me off."

"And you like to be shown off," Marissa observed. An associate at a large midtown law firm, Dana was always conservatively dressed for work, but, knowing Dana as she did, it was no real stretch to imagine the self-proclaimed sub girl dressed in something skimpy and provocative at a private club.

"It pleases my Master, and that pleases me," Dana said simply.

"Oh," Marissa breathed, Dana's words resonating somewhere deep inside her. Again the daydream of belonging to another in the deepest sense of the word threatened to engulf Marissa, and she felt herself drifting to that dark, secret place.

There was a soft knock at the door, and the sound released Marissa from the erotic spell she'd been falling into. "Someone at my door. Gotta go," she said. "See you tonight."

"See ya!" Dana sang into the phone.

Marissa took a moment to compose herself. She touched the plastic rectangle above her breast that read *Dr. Roberts*. Feeling centered again, she called out, "Come in."

The door opened and the handsome new nurse stuck his head into the office. Marissa was glad the lab coat covered her still perking nipples. "Yes?" she said in her best professional doctor voice. "Cam, is it?" As if she didn't know. As if he weren't the primary topic of conversation at the nurses' station whenever he wasn't around.

"Yes, Dr. Roberts. If you had a minute, I wanted to talk to you about Mr. Santana in room two thirteen. I have some suggestions that might be useful." He stood just inside the door, looking like some kind of GQ model for hospital scrubs, a chart tucked underneath one of his tan, muscular arms. His eyes really were remarkably blue, especially in contrast to his dark brown hair. And those lips. What would it be like to kiss those lips?

What the fuck? He was a nurse, for crying out loud. Not some sex object for Marissa to ogle. Embarrassed, she gestured toward a chair in front of her desk. "Please, have a seat."

As Cam sat across from her, Marissa couldn't stop herself from staring into those deep, kind eyes. Something about the man was so compelling she had to physically restrain herself to keep from leaping over the desk and into his lap. Jesus H Christ, she must be farther gone than she realized. Now she was lusting after gay guys.

Okay, stop it this instant. You're an MD. A professional. Act like it.

Marissa leaned forward and held out her hand for the chart. His fingers brushed hers as she took the chart from him, and though she knew it was all in her mind, the electric spark that passed between them shot straight to her pussy. It was all she could do not to gasp, and she prayed her voice would come out steady.

She lifted her chin, reminding herself she was the doctor here. "Tell me what's going on with Mr. Santana," she said crisply.

Chapter 2

When the taxi pulled up to the curb of Marissa's apartment building, a man in jeans and a black T-shirt beneath a sports jacket climbed out of the backseat. "Hey there, you must be Marissa. I'm Tony. Great to meet you at last." His voice was deep and seemed too large for the rest of him.

"Oh, hi. Nice to meet you too." Marissa took the man's offered hand. She had always envisioned Tony as a big, burly man in black leather and black army boots, like Master Mark on her favorite videos. It took her a second to readjust her mental image of Dana's Master/husband. He was looking her over as well, his eyes moving with an appreciative gaze from her face, to her breasts, to her legs and back up again. Normally Marissa would have taken offense at a man regarding her with such brazen scrutiny, but somehow with Tony it didn't offend. She found herself hoping instead that he was pleased with what he saw.

After much deliberation and the trying and discarding of a number of outfits, Marissa had finally settled on the first thing she'd pulled from the closet—a simple sleeveless black dress she had spent too much on, but which hugged her curves in all the right places. It was lower cut than what she usually wore, but she was going to a BDSM sex club, after all, so why not? Judging from Tony's appreciative gaze, he approved.

Tony waved toward the open car door. "After you," he said. Marissa preceded him into the roomy backseat of the old-fashioned yellow cab.

"Hey, girlfriend!" Dana, already seated, enthused as Marissa settled herself between the couple. She would have preferred to be on Dana's other side, rather than separating the pair, but neither of them seemed the slightest perturbed by this.

As the cab pulled away, Marissa turned to her friend to see what she was wearing, but a light spring coat covered her outfit. Dana's auburn hair, usually pulled back during the workday, fell in a shiny curtain to her shoulders. Unlike the conservative makeup she wore while practicing law, Dana's eyes were heavily made up with eyeliner and mascara and her lips were painted a deep, shiny red.

Dana leaned back against her car door as she appraised Marissa. "I love the dress," she said. "Though it would look even better without a bra, don't you agree, Tony?"

Tony slid his arm over the back of the car seat. "I do indeed. Perhaps a punishment is in order for daring to harness such luscious breasts."

Marissa stiffened with embarrassment and felt her face flush. What the hell? Dana might belong to Master Tony, but Marissa sure as hell didn't. She barely knew the guy! She opened her mouth in protest, but before she could speak, both Dana and

Tony laughed, and Dana reached for Marissa's hand. "We're just teasing, silly. I'm sorry. You'll have to forgive our sense of humor."

"Yeah," Tony agreed, still chuckling. "We're so used to hanging out with other folks into the scene, we sometimes forget to take the tender feelings of newbies into account."

"Newbies, huh," Marissa countered, trying to put a cocky edge into her tone. "So you two do this a lot? Find young innocents to corrupt?"

"As often as we can," Dana quipped.

"Seriously, though," Tony added. "We do regard it as a kind of sacred duty to help people who are curious about the lifestyle to find their way. There's a lot of misinformation out there about BDSM. Did you know you can still go to jail or lose custody of your children in some states, just for practicing consensual BDSM sex in the privacy of your own home? Even though BDSM has moved more into the mainstream over the past few years, there's still a lot of confusion about consensual power exchanges, and the passion and commitment that's required. Sometimes it seems like we take two steps forward and one step back when it comes to freedom of sexual expression in this country."

"You got that right," Dana added, her tone suddenly dark. "Certain distribution websites that shall remain nameless have even started censoring BDSM erotica, if you can believe it. That's one reason we love The Power Exchange. It's a safe place to practice our kink with likeminded people who *get* it."

"I really appreciate your including me tonight," Marissa said. "Though I'm kind of nervous. I won't, you know, like, be expected to *do* anything, will I?"

Dana laughed and squeezed Marissa's leg. "Only if you want to."

Marissa thought about this as the cab wended its way through city traffic toward the lower west side of Manhattan. A sudden vision of herself naked, her arms extended high over her head, her legs spread and chained to the floor by shackles around her ankles, flashed into her brain. She felt a tingle in her pussy as Master Mark appeared behind her in the video now playing in her overactive imagination. He was holding a heavy flogger, and it cracked against Marissa's skin with each stinging stroke. He moved closer behind her, nuzzling his mouth against her neck as he reached around with his free hand to squeeze her breast.

Marissa sat up straighter and glanced at Dana and Tony, suddenly afraid her lusty little daydream was somehow apparent to them. But they were both looking out their respective windows at the lights of the city passing by. Marissa smoothed back her hair, which she had worn loose for the evening, and blew out a cleansing breath.

After about ten minutes, they pulled onto a dark street that contained a row of what looked like abandoned warehouses. The cab pulled to the curb and the cabbie twisted back. "This the place, Mac?"

"The very one," Tony replied with a smile. He handed some bills to the cabbie and opened the car door to step out onto the sidewalk. Wearing heels higher than she was used to, Marissa gratefully accepted Tony's offered hand as she climbed out of the car.

He helped out Dana as well, who, in her heels, stood a good three inches taller than her spouse. Finally he opened the front passenger door of the cab and pulled out a large black leather messenger bag, which he slung over his shoulder.

As the cab pulled away, Tony walked toward a metal door and pressed a buzzer beside it. Dana and Marissa stood just behind him. "This is the club?" Marissa said quietly to her friend, unable to keep the skepticism from her voice. The place looked like a dump. The images she had earlier of a dank, stone dungeon with manacles protruding from the walls resurfaced with a vengeance in her mind. What in god's name had she signed up for?

"Not to worry," Dana said as if reading her mind. She reached for Marissa's hand and gave it a squeeze. "It's much nicer inside."

A voice came over the intercom asking them to state their business. "Master Tony, slave Dana and guest," Tony said in his deep voice.

Slave Dana.

The words sent a shiver down Marissa's spine. Would she ever be someone's sex slave? Did she want to be?

No, her mind insisted. *No way.*

Yes, her body whispered fervently.

The door buzzed and Tony pulled it open, gesturing for the women to enter ahead of him. A set of wide stairs led downward, and the clacking of the women's heels echoed against the concrete walls. Marissa held tight to the metal railing as they descended. There was a second door at the bottom of the stairs, which was pulled open as they approached.

A wiry young man with short blond hair dressed wearing only black leather pants and a slave collar ushered them inside. He was holding a clipboard, and he checked something off and looked at them with a smile. "Welcome, Master Tony," he said, not even glancing toward Dana or Marissa.

"Good evening, Steven," Tony replied. Marissa noticed Steven's nipples were pierced, small silver barbells gleaming against his smooth chest.

A young woman with long dark hair hanging loose down her back appeared. She was wearing a sheer white dress made of a kind of stretchy lace fabric that did little to hide the fact she was completely nude beneath it. Her feet were bare, and she wore a thick metal chain around her neck. "Lovely to see you, slave Jade," Tony said.

"Good evening, Sir," the girl replied in a quiet, respectful tone. An involuntary shudder moved through Marissa's frame and her nipples poked hard against the lace of her bra as her mind replaced Jade's name with her own.

The young woman led the three of them to a table at the far side of the room, and as they walked, Marissa took in her surroundings. She was quite impressed with the opulence of the place, especially considering the façade of the seemingly rundown building in the nearly deserted neighborhood that housed it. Instead of a medieval stone dungeon, the space looked more like a posh Westchester County country club. The lighting was softly muted, the walls painted a warm, creamy beige, the thickly piled carpeting a soft tan. Instead of iron manacles, oil paintings of lush landscapes and plump, nude women lounging on velvet settees were hung along the walls. Leather sofas and deep, plush chairs were scattered throughout the room in conversational arrangements, and half a dozen small tables were set up near a long bar of polished wood and brass. Soft classical music filled the room, though Marissa couldn't see evidence of any speakers.

That was where the comparison to a country club ended, however. Large circles had been cut into the carpet in various spots around the spacious room, and equipment Marissa recognized from the online BDSM training site was set up in each circle. These included whipping posts, medical exam tables, large X crosses and spanking benches.

"Those are the punishment circles," Dana explained, following Marissa's wide-eyed gaze. "That's where people do public scenes, as you can see."

Marissa could barely keep her mouth from hanging open as she struggled to process everything going on around her. As Dana had warned, there were both women and men in various states of undress. A rather large woman brushed by Marissa as they walked toward their table. She was wearing a black leather bustier cinched in at the waist, her ample breasts spilling out over the top. There was a guy in his forties who was completely naked, save for a small cage fitted over his genitals. His hands were loosely cuffed to a thick leather collar around his neck, and he was being led on a leash by a tall, imposing woman with impossibly high heels wearing a full-length black velvet gown.

A man with a black hood covering his head and face was kneeling on all fours between two seated women, both of whom were resting their stiletto-heeled feet on his bare back and talking over him as if he were no more than a piece of furniture.

A naked woman was bound to a whipping post in one of the punishment circles, a black blindfold over her eyes, her ass bright red and mottled with bruises. Another woman dressed in a very short black leather skirt and a sheer white silk blouse stood just behind her, smacking the woman's ass with a long-handled purple riding crop.

A woman was lying face-up an exam table, her wrists and ankles buckled down at the corners with leather restraints. Four men were gathered around her, each holding a lit candle. Her naked body was covered in splattered red wax, especially her pubic area and breasts, and she whimpered softly each time more droplets of melted wax scalded her skin.

Neither Tony nor Dana seemed the slightest bit perturbed by any of this as they wove their way through the small crowds clustered around each scene. It was all Marissa could do to keep moving beside them, when all she really wanted to do was stop and stare.

Once they got to their table, Tony pulled out chairs for both Marissa and Dana. He stood behind Dana and helped her remove her coat. Beneath the coat, Dana wore a dark green satin corset cinched tightly at her long, slender waist. Her small breasts were pushed high in the bodice of the corset, which was cut so low the top half of her pink nipples were showing. She wore a skirt of matching green leather that barely covered the tops of her slender thighs. Marissa knew from seeing her in the gym locker room that Dana was shaved smooth, and she found herself wondering if she was wearing any underwear. Though Dana had a killer body, still Marissa marveled at her friend's apparent ease and confidence at displaying herself like that in public.

Yet she had to admit Dana looked spectacular, the effect far sexier than if she'd been merely naked. The deep green of the corset set off her green eyes and auburn hair, and her breasts looked like perfect, ripe peaches, bunched together and just waiting to be tasted.

"You look stunning," Marissa breathed, feeling dowdy in comparison in her black cocktail dress.

"Thank you." Dana smiled brightly. "Master Tony brought home this lovely corset this afternoon."

Tony stroked his wife's arm, and Marissa could see the love in his eyes. "A gift for my slave girl," he said. Turning to Marissa, he added, "She'll earn it tonight." Leaning down, he reached for the messenger bag he'd set on the floor beside his chair and opened the flap. He pulled out a black plastic container and placed it on the table.

At that moment, a young woman wearing nothing but a black satin apron with a huge bow at the back appeared beside their table, a small order pad and pen in her hand. Her chest and arms were covered in an elaborate series of tattoos and large gold hoops dangled from her nipples.

"The usual, Sir?" she asked Tony, not even glancing at Dana or Marissa.

Tony turned to Marissa. "Do you drink champagne, Marissa?"

"Yes. I love champagne," Marissa said, though she was a little confused by the question.

Tony turned back to the nearly naked waitress. "Yes, Stella," he said with a nod. "Three mimosas over crushed ice."

Stella did a small curtsey. "Yes, Sir. Right away."

"I thought there was no alcohol allowed at BDSM clubs," Marissa said, having heard this somewhere or other.

"Not at public clubs," Tony agreed. "And yes, as a rule, you don't want to mix alcohol with BDSM play. But one glass of champagne won't hurt us."

"And they squeeze their orange juice fresh," Dana added. "I always have to have at least one mimosa when we come to the club. The champagne is almost an afterthought."

"Okay, sounds great." After all, Marissa certainly wasn't planning to engage in any BDSM play. And a drink might take the edge off her nerves.

After the waitress left them, Marissa nodded toward the container Tony had placed on the table. "What's that?"

Tony turned the clasp and opened the lid, revealing a black plastic wand with a red tip, and three glass rods, one with a round flat end like a stethoscope, one shaped like a large comb and one shaped like a dental implement.

"What is all that?" Marissa asked.

"It's a violet wand kit," Dana said, her eyes literally glowing with delight as she stared at the toys. Marissa had heard of this type of BDSM sex toy, but she'd never actually seen one. "That's like electrical shock, right? Isn't that dangerous?"

Dana shook her head. "Not if it's handled correctly." She smiled warmly at her husband and then stroked one of the glass rods. "At a low setting it feels like tiny champagne bubbles fizzing on your skin. Increase the intensity, and it can be quite a shock."

Marissa bit her lip. "Yikes. That's got to hurt."

"That's the idea, silly. It hurts *so* good." Dana grinned but then sobered. "Seriously, though. It's not really pain, per se. It's more like intensity. And that's what we masochists crave the most. Intensity of experience. Pain is just one aspect of intensity."

While Marissa thought about this, Tony added, "The wand delivers a spray of electrical sparks onto your skin that excite your nerve endings." He picked up the black plastic wand and fitted the glass rod with the stethoscope end into the head of the wand.

"They operate on a low current, high voltage, high frequency electricity to the body," he continued. He flipped a small switch at the base of the wand and held the glass head close to Dana's arm. The glass turned a bright purple, tiny sparks of electricity like bolts of lightning flying from the head. "Oooh," Dana said, shivering, while Marissa gasped in surprise at the unexpected fireworks. It was really quite beautiful.

"Contrary to what you might think," Tony said as he held the wand a few inches away from Dana's arm, "the farther you hold the electrode from your partner's skin, the sharper the shock." A small crack of electricity cut the air between them as the wand flashed purple and white, and Dana uttered a small squeal.

Tony removed the glass electrode and set it carefully back into its foam slot. He reached again into the messenger bag and took out a small, thin-handled whip. Instead of the usual leather, the strands were made of some kind of bright blue material, almost like the fiber optic rods of a light sculpture. "This," he said with a cruel, sensual smile as he ran his fingers through the blue strands, "is how slave Dana's going to earn her new corset."

"Oh," Marissa said softly, the word escaping unbidden from her lips as she watched Tony fit the whip handle into the plastic wand.

"This particular flogger," he explained, "is made for use with a violet wand. The electrical charge is conducted evenly through each of the forty-five strands of Mylar, delivering an intense prickling sensation on contact. Tonight Dana is going to submit to an electrical flogging, aren't you, darling?"

"Yes, Sir," Dana breathed, her eyes shining.

The waitress reappeared with their drinks, and Marissa was glad for the distraction. She felt both agitated and deeply excited by the heady atmosphere of the club, and by the erotically-charged connection that existed between Dana and her Master/husband. Dana hadn't expressly said she was going to scene with her Master that evening, though Marissa supposed she should have expected it.

The couple moved their heads together until their foreheads were touching. The gesture was somehow more intimate than even a kiss would have been. As Marissa watched them, a vague, undefined longing swept through her, and she thought about Dana's earlier analogy likening her to a kid with her face pressed up against the glass of a candy store. But this was more than candy, she understood now. For Dana and Tony, and maybe for her as well, this was sustenance of the most basic kind, and she, Marissa, had been unwittingly starved for it all her life.

Their silent, intense communication completed, Tony and Dana leaned away from each other. Marissa looked quickly away so as not to be caught staring. When she reached for her glass, she saw her hand was shaking slightly. Looking up, she met Dana's eye. Dana smiled kindly. "I'm really proud of you, Marissa. I know this whole scene is a lot to process for a sub-curious girl like you. Coming here is the first step to a whole new life, if you want it."

Tony lifted his glass, and the women followed suit. As they clinked, he said, "To the two loveliest sub girls in Manhattan. Now, let's go play!"

Chapter 3

Late Saturday morning Cam jogged up the steps from the subway and headed along St. Mark's Place. The heavyset woman waving wildly at him from across the street looked familiar, though it took Cam a moment to place her. Janice was an RN at the hospital who, Cam had already figured out, was something of a gossip, her head always leaned conspiratorially close to a colleague, her eyes darting knowingly as she spread the latest rumor. Cam waved back and continued walking. He could still feel the woman's eyes on him. He briefly considered moving past his destination, but decided at the last second not to. What the hell, he'd give the old girl something else to whisper about at the water cooler.

He went down the three steps that led to the door of the boutique. A male mannequin was featured in the window, decked out in leather and chains, a bright red ball gag fitted over his mouth beneath vacant, staring eyes.

A little bell jingled as Cam entered the small space and Celia looked up from behind the counter, her face splitting into a broad grin. "Hey there, stranger. It's been way too long. Where've you been? I was afraid maybe you'd found a better place to get your gear. Maybe even online, god forbid."

Celia's hair was pink today, gelled into a crown of spiky points around her head that matched the metal spikes of her dog collar. She wore a black, very low cut leather bustier and when she stepped out from behind the counter Cam saw the rest of her ensemble—a pink satin miniskirt and high black leather boots. Somehow on her, it worked. She held out her arms and Cam moved into her embrace, leaning down to give her a quick kiss on the cheek.

"I would never abandon you, Celia, you know that. You and Cat are my go-to girls for all my gear. I've just been really busy, is all. I got a new job and I've had to pull a few weekend shifts as the new kid on the block."

"Okay, then," Celia said with a mollified nod. "What can I do for you today?"

"I'm interested in a new flogger. Something in leather, not suede. I need something with more sting. And I could use a couple more canes. I broke one the other day."

"On somebody's ass?"

Cam nodded. "Yeah. The guy had buns of steel and kept telling me to hit him harder. He could definitely take it, but obviously the cane couldn't. "

"Oooh, lucky guy." Celia moved closer again. "You can break a cane on my ass anytime you like, sugar," she purred teasingly.

"Somehow I don't think Mistress Cat would approve," Cam teased back.

"Ah, but she's out of town. And you know what they say…when the cat's away…"

Cam just shook his head, though he was smiling. Celia loved to flirt, but she was one hundred percent gay and never scened with men, period. "Okay, okay," Celia said, pretending defeat. "If I can't get you to cane me, at least I can get you to buy something. Let me show you what we've got. I have some fabulous new floggers by Adam Sands, that Australian dude who does everything by hand."

Cam took his time examining the floggers, weighing the workmanship and quality of the leather against cost as he tried to make his selection. The club actually provided gear to its Master Trainers, of which Cam was one, but he liked to have his own things, especially when it came to flogging. A good flogger became the extension of your arm, almost a part of you, and an intimate knowledge of its heft, balance and stroke was essential in Cam's book.

Someday, he thought with a sudden wistfulness, he would find his own sub girl, and together they would choose their own gear, gear they would keep at home. This girl, no, this woman, would be strong and confident, successful in her professional life and happy in herself, but sexually submissive to Cam. She was out there somewhere, he knew she was, and he was willing to wait for her.

He'd had several D/s relationships with women over the years, some more successful than others, none that lasted beyond a few months. He'd pretty much run the gamut, from super intense to nearly vanilla. On one end of the spectrum was Nicole. With her, the BDSM sex had been hot, and there was no erotic torture he could devise that she didn't fully embrace. It had been great, at first, but after a while Nicole had needed more—more than he was willing or able to give. She wanted him to shave her head and to brand her ass with his initials. She wanted to sleep in a box underneath his bed in shackles. She wanted him to use her as his toilet, and to verbally humiliate her while he pissed into her mouth. While he understood her deep-seated need for such complete and total objectification, that wasn't what he was looking for, and he had to break things off.

Then there was Coleen, beautiful, vivacious and smart as a whip. She'd seemed excited and eager when he'd first introduced the concept of BDSM play into their sex life. But eventually he'd figured out that for her it was just a game, a fun kink that proved how sexually free and open she was. When Cam tried to take it deeper, she balked and ran, and he let her go, aware she wasn't the one.

Over the years he'd found himself pulling back from seeking a love match with a submissive woman, or any woman for that matter. It wasn't that he didn't want love, but he'd decided to let it find him. When the connection was right, he'd know it. Meanwhile, he had the club, and the satisfaction he derived from training. For now, that was enough.

~*~

Janice and Lawanda were whispering as Marissa approached the counter. They pulled apart when they saw her and Janice hurried away. Marissa took the stack of charts and sat down behind the counter to type in her notes at a terminal. From behind her, Lawanda said, "You'll never guess Janice's latest juicy tidbit."

Marissa snorted. "Come on, Lawanda, whatever it is, please consider the source. According to Janice, the chief of oncology is having an affair with any number of the nurses, Frank down in the mailroom is really a CIA operative, and I've secretly been married and divorced three times."

"Wait," Lawanda said with mock surprise. "You mean you haven't?"

Marissa laughed and shook her head. She tried to focus on her work but Lawanda persisted. "It's about Cam Wilder."

Marissa didn't turn around, but her fingers stilled on the keyboard. "Oh?" she said in an elaborately casual tone. Shit, even the guy's name was enough to make her tingle.

Lawanda laughed knowingly. "Yeah, oh," she agreed. "The verdict is in on our newest hunk. This isn't even gossip, it's just the facts. Janice has proof. She *saw* him on Saturday going into one of those gay sex shops down in the Village. It's official. The guy is queer as a two-dollar bill."

"Oh," Marissa said again, her heart plummeting into her shoes. She forced a small laugh and shrugged. "Just as well," she lied. "Less distraction for the ladies, right?"

The busy day finally came to an end, and Marissa considered canceling her evening plans so she could take a hot bath and go to bed early. But she was only kidding herself. No way was she going to cancel. She had to see this through. She just had to.

Since Friday night at the club with Tony and Dana, Marissa hadn't been able to stop thinking about what she'd witnessed. Watching Tony whip Dana with the electric flogger had been an extraordinary experience. Marissa had hugged herself as she watched, barely able to keep from whimpering with longing. Dana had been quiet at first, but as the flogging intensified and the sparks flew, she'd begun to yelp and squirm, and Marissa could almost feel the electric sting of the strands as they whipped over her friend's bare back and ass. Then Dana had quieted again, though Tony had continued to flog her, if anything harder than before. A stillness had moved over Dana's body and her face had been suffused with a kind of ethereal glow that was hard to describe.

Finally Tony had set down the flogger and released his wife from the large X-shaped cross to which he had earlier bound her by the wrists and ankles. She fell back into his arms without looking, her trust complete that he would catch her, which of course he did. Though he was the smaller of the two, he was apparently quite strong. He lifted her effortlessly into his arms and carried her to one of a series of sofas set around the room, Marissa forgotten. She'd trailed along, not wanting to intrude, but not sure what else to do.

Eventually Dana had opened her eyes and fixed Marissa with an angelic smile. "Hi," she'd said. "So what did you think?"

Never in her life had Marissa yearned for something so fiercely, not even in her certainty since elementary school that she wanted to be a doctor. Seeing Dana, someone she knew and loved, transported by the erotic experience, had sealed the deal in her mind. She was done being a voyeur, watching videos and dreaming her secret dreams in the dark. She was ready for more. "I want it," Marissa had blurted before realizing she was going to speak. "I want what you have."

"Then you shall have it," Tony had answered.

And tonight was the night. Dana had called her on Sunday to invite her over for what Tony had called "an exploration of your submissive potential." Marissa's heart had kicked immediately into high gear at the offer, but she was on call until six a.m. Monday and so had to decline. In a way she had been almost relieved to have a good excuse. Maybe she wasn't as ready as she'd thought that night in the club.

"How about tomorrow night, then?" Dana had persisted, and again the longing had surfaced, as powerful and persistent as before.

Still, she forced herself to respond cautiously. "Um, what exactly are we talking about?"

"Whatever works for you," Dana had replied breezily. "Tony and I are very comfortable scening with others, but we get it that you're new to all this. If you just want to see what it feels like to maybe be tied up and spanked, we can do that. Or we can go further. It's totally up to you."

"At the club?" Marissa asked hopefully.

Dana shook her head. "Sorry. Open invitation night is only once a month."

"Oh." Marissa was surprised by how much this news deflated her. She wanted to go back. She wanted to be immersed in the heady, intense atmosphere of the luxurious, exotic surroundings of The Power Exchange. When they'd dropped her at home late Friday night, she'd masturbated in bed to images of herself in one of those punishment circles, naked and chained to a cross, a strong, faceless man whipping her until she begged for mercy. She'd moaned aloud when the man had pressed his naked body to hers, his erect cock hard against the small of her back. He'd released her from the cross and pushed her to the floor, where he'd mounted and fucked her until she screamed once more for mercy. She'd come hard, there alone in the dark.

"It's better to take this first step in a private space, rather than a public club," Dana had assured her. "It's one thing to fantasize, but it could be you just like the *idea* of erotic torture and submission. Physically it might not be right for you. This is a way to dip your toe in, if you will, to see how your body reacts to what your mind thinks it craves."

That made sense to Marissa, and she had genuinely liked Tony. Plus, Tony and Dana were clearly in love. This wasn't just an excuse for the husband in a relationship to touch another woman, at least she was pretty sure it wasn't. Just the same, she'd said, "I can keep my clothes on, right?"

"We'll figure it out when you get here," Dana had replied evasively, but then she'd added with a laugh, "Don't worry, girlfriend. Whatever we work out, it will be with your full and complete consent. See you at eight. Be there or be square."

Dana and Tony lived in a nice apartment building right off Central Park West in the seventies, complete with a doorman, who checked his iPad for Marissa's name before granting her access to the marbled lobby. The elevator stopped on their floor and Marissa stepped out, feeling as nervous as a teenager on her first date. She rang the doorbell at number 1218 and stepped back.

A moment later the door opened and there stood her friend Dana. "Welcome. Come in, come in." She pulled Marissa into a hug and then let her go.

Marissa took in the clean, elegant lines of the living room, with dark hardwood floors, minimalist leather and chrome furniture and a huge flat screen TV against one wall. The Manhattan skyline unfolded in a breathtaking view outside a huge picture window. Marissa's entire apartment would fit into this one room, she realized. Both Dana and Tony were attorneys, Tony a partner at his firm. Clearly law paid better than medicine, she thought with an inward shrug. "What a gorgeous place," she said sincerely.

"Thanks. We like it."

Tony appeared from what must be the kitchen. He was holding a bottle of red wine and three glasses. "Hey there, Marissa. Welcome." He moved toward a sofa with a coffee table set in front of it and put down the wine. "Come sit down. We'll share a glass and talk about expectations, okay?"

Dana and she moved to sit down. Dana was wearing a white loose-flowing shift, her small, high breasts braless beneath the sheer fabric, her feet bare. Tony was wearing black jeans and a black T-shirt. Marissa was glad she'd changed from her work clothes into a silk batik tank top and white slacks.

Dana and Marissa sat on the sofa, and Tony sat across from them in a chair. He poured the wine and handed each woman a glass. Marissa took a sip. It was delicious, and she took another, letting its warmth move through her. After a bit of small talk, Tony put down his glass and stood. He moved around the table and, as Dana shifted to the side, sat down between the two women.

Marissa's heart picked up its pace as Tony turned toward her. He reached for her hand, and Marissa let him take it. "Nothing that happens tonight will happen without your full consent. Dana and I have talked it over, and we would like to introduce you to a little light bondage and maybe a spanking or a flogging, depending on your comfort level. Does that sound good to you?"

Marissa's mouth had gone dry and her voice came out hoarse when she answered. "Yes," she managed, shocking herself by adding, "please."

Tony smiled and let go of her hand. He stood. "Good. Why don't you two go along to the playroom? I'll join you in a moment." Marissa darted a look at Dana, who had stood as well and was smiling. Finishing her wine, Marissa placed her glass on the table and got up, her heart beating with nervous anticipation.

While Tony took the bottle and glasses back into the kitchen, Dana led Marissa through the living room and down a narrow hallway, stopping at a closed door. Dana opened the door and stepped inside, clicking on the light as she entered. Marissa followed. Inside the room was a mini version of the club, complete with a cross, a spanking bench and, intriguingly, a human-size cage in the corner of the room. One wall was hung with coils of rope and various whips, canes and floggers. All sorts of cuffs, gags and other BDSM paraphernalia were set out on a long, high table against the back wall. Tucked into a corner was a plump loveseat with deep cushions, a small pile of blankets and towels stacked neatly on an end table beside it.

"Wow," Marissa whispered, her mouth hanging open as she took in the space.

"Pretty amazing, huh?" Dana enthused. "Am I the luckiest girl in the world, or what?" Then, to Marissa's surprise, Dana pulled the shift over her head and hung it on a hook just inside the door. Completely naked, she dropped to her knees on a small mat just inside the door and locked her arms behind her back, thrusting her small, perfect breasts proudly forward.

Seeing Marissa's shocked expression, she said, "I'm sorry, I should have warned you. I must always strip immediately when I enter Master's playroom. It puts me in what Master Tony calls a proper frame of mind." Dana's voice had taken on a sultry, husky tone, and she already had that dreamy expression on her face Marissa had seen at the club.

"Oh," Marissa replied inanely.

Tony appeared in the door. He stepped in front of his kneeling wife and bent down to kiss the top of her head. Turning to Marissa he said in a matter-of-fact tone, "Would you like to start on the spanking bench or on the cross?"

"Um, gosh. I don't know."

"Would you like me to decide for you?" Like Dana, Tony's voice had also taken on a deeper timbre, and he seemed to radiate a kind of mastery Marissa found extremely attractive.

"Uh, yeah. Yes. That would be good."

"Yes, Sir," Tony corrected. "While in this room, you will call me Master, or Sir, understood?"

Something lit deep in Marissa's gut at these words, a tiny but bright flame of desire. "Yes," she breathed. "Yes, Sir."

Tony nodded. "We'll go with the St. Andrew's cross. Face the cross and lift your arms against the X. I will strap you into place."

Marissa felt like she was in a kind of dream as she moved toward the cross. She leaned against the large wooden X and lifted her arms. "I'm going to take off your sandals, okay?" Tony said.

"Yes, Sir."

Tony crouched behind her and unbuckled her sandals, slipping each one off. Something about the gesture was both masterful and tender, and Marissa realized she was deeply attracted to Dana's husband, and not quite sure how she felt about that. Tony moved just behind her, the warmth of his body seeping through her clothing as he reached up and strapped one wrist and then the other against the smooth, polished wood of the cross.

A shudder moved through her frame, shaking her to her core as the leather cuffs closed snugly around her wrists. The sense of vulnerability was nearly overwhelming, but at the same time her entire being thrilled to the sensation of being bound.

She jumped when Tony lightly caressed her back. "Relax," he murmured into her ear. "How are you doing? You okay?"

Marissa nodded, both confused and excited by what was happening to her.

"While in this room, Marissa, you are my sub girl. My sub girl will answer all questions with words. It's important that I hear you speak, and it's also a sign of respect. So I'll ask again. Are you okay?"

Sub girl.

The words resonated deep inside Marissa. "Yes, Sir," she whispered, her heart beating high in her throat. "I'm okay, Sir. I'm good."

"Good." He stepped back and moved so Marissa could see his face. "Not that I think you'll need it for this exercise, but it's always a good idea to have a safeword, especially between people who aren't intimately familiar with one another. Do you know what a safeword is?"

"Yes, I think so, uh, Sir," Marissa answered. "It's a word I would use if the scene got too intense. If I needed all the action to stop."

Tony nodded. "That's correct. It's a word that we would never mistake as being an ongoing part of the scene. Something random, but that you would easily remember. Dana's safeword is banana. Do you want to select a piece of fruit?" He grinned.

"Um. I'll take lemon," Marissa replied, deciding not to make a Freudian joke of Dana's particular selection. Then the import of what she'd just done, of what she was doing, really hit her. A safeword!

"Lemon," Tony repeated matter-of-factly, unaware of the turmoil going on inside Marissa's head. "Perfect." He stepped again behind her. "I'm going to leave your legs free for now. I think we'll start with a spanking, just to get a sense of what you can handle. Pants on or off?"

Marissa swallowed, thinking of Dana naked behind her and so comfortable in her nudity. But Dana and Tony were married, and Dana was a bona fide sub girl, while Marissa was still only sub-curious, and really barely knew Tony. "Pants on...Sir."

"All right, but feel free to change your mind. I'm going to spank you now."

Marissa squeezed her eyes shut and tensed with nervous anticipation. Tony's palm landed with a smack against her ass and Marissa gasped more out of surprise than anything. He struck her several more times in succession. Marissa began to relax. This wasn't so bad. In fact, she had to admit she kind of liked the thud of his hard hand against her ass.

"How are you doing?" Tony asked.

"Good, Sir," Marissa said. "But, um..." Did she dare?

"Yes?"

"Could we maybe try it with the pants off, but panties on?"

Tony chuckled. "We could do that."

"It's best skin on skin, Marissa, sweetheart," Dana chimed in. "Don't be shy. Tony's seen bare bottoms before, trust me."

Marissa said nothing to this. She drew in a tremulous breath as Tony unzipped the side zipper on her summer slacks and pulled them down her legs.

"We continue," Tony said from behind her. His hand made more of an impact now, with only the thin silk of her panties between them. Marissa gasped as the sting mounted and her flesh heated. She began to pant, and became aware of the throb of her clit and the dampness in the crotch of her underwear.

He struck her hard, his rhythm steady as he covered every inch of her bottom. Tears stung her eyelids and Marissa began to dance a little on her toes, her body twisting to avoid Tony's hard, relentless palm.

"I smell your desire," Tony announced from behind her, and Marissa felt her face flame at these words.

"Oh, god," she moaned, the words ripped from her mouth without her permission.

"No god." Tony chuckled. "Just me. Are you ready for skin on skin, sub girl?"

Her tongue felt thick in her mouth and she could barely hear over the pounding of her own heart. "Skin, Sir," she finally managed. He yanked down the flimsy, sex-soaked silk and pulled it away.

The solid impact of his hand against her ass sent another spasm through Marissa's frame, this one as much pure, raw lust as fear. She began to pant. Her nipples actually hurt and her clit throbbed so hard she felt like she might actually come without being touched, if such a thing were possible. "Oh, god," she heard herself moan again, though the voice seemed disembodied, as if it belonged to someone else. Her ass was on fire, her cunt was soaked in liquid heat, her mind was short-circuiting, her heart smashing wildly against the confines of her ribcage. "Oh, god, oh, god, oh, god," she chanted as Tony struck her again, and again, and again.

Then it happened—as impossible as it seemed, Marissa felt the familiar warm, buttery clutch of an orgasm rising deep in her belly and shuddering through her body as she gasped and jerked against her wrist restraints. Finally she sagged against the cross, tears streaming down her cheeks, blood roaring in her ears, her breath rasping in her throat.

After a while—a second, a minute, an eternity, who could say?—she heard Tony's dry chuckle behind her, and she realized the spanking had stopped. She felt him reach for one wrist and then the other, releasing the Velcro straps that held her in place. She fell back against him, her eyes closed as she reveled in the warmth of his strong embrace.

Tony put a supportive arm around Marissa's shoulders and led her to the loveseat, where Dana now waited, a blanket spread open on her lap. As Tony eased Marissa onto the loveseat, Dana wrapped the blanket around her shoulders. Marissa leaned against her friend, who pulled her close. She rested her head on Dana's shoulder, her eyes closing of their own accord as a happy sigh escaped her lips.

"This girl is natural," Tony said from somewhere in the distance. "No question about it. She was born to submit."

Chapter 4

Dr. Roberts was discussing the medical treatment plans for Cam's patients, and Cam was mostly paying attention, but her mouth kept distracting him. It was a sensual mouth, her lips mobile and expressive as she spoke. She had a sexy voice, too, slightly husky while still completely feminine. He liked that she didn't wear a lot of makeup—just a bit of mascara and a hint of pink lip-gloss, as far as he could tell. Her glossy hair was pulled back in a wide barrette at the nape of her neck, as it always was at work. What would it look like loose, tendrils curling around her face?

Her skin looked dewy fresh, and he had an irrational urge to stroke her cheek, just to see if it was as soft as it appeared. In spite of his best intentions to focus, his overactive libido kept inserting images of this beautiful woman kneeling naked in front of him and parting those luscious lips to receive the head of his cock. He would just give her the head at first. She would have to earn more.

She was asking a question about medications and Cam gave himself a mental shake. As his mouth responded to her question, his brain demanded to know what the fuck his problem was. Marissa Roberts was a doctor, for crying out loud, not to mention they worked together. Anyway, she was probably vanilla as an ice cream cone, and because of that, even if the sex was fantastic, it could never be more than a one-night stand. And he no longer did one-night stands. Especially not with vanilla MDs who looked down their noses at male nurses. Not that she'd ever offered the slightest hint of disrespect, but Cam was hypersensitive to the mutterings of hospital staff, and why should she be any different? Even though it was the twenty-first century, male nurses were still considered somewhat suspect, which was ironic, when you thought about it.

He forced himself back to his duties, thankfully easing once more into professional mode as they discussed the caseload for the week. Their meeting completed, Dr. Roberts turned and walked briskly away. He couldn't stop himself from gazing after her as she headed toward the elevator bank. Again his imagination slipped into forbidden territory, as it removed the white lab coat and sensible pumps, re-dressing her in stiletto heels, stocking and garters, and nothing else. Before his body got into the act and gave him an erection, Cam turned back to his computer screen and busied himself with typing up his notes. The weekend, after all, was only a few hours away.

~*~

"Okay, I worked it out. You're in."

"You did?" Marissa realized her voice had come out as a squeak. She cleared her throat. "So I can come to the club with you tonight even though it's not an open invitation night?" Marissa jumped up from her desk and did a little happy dance before catching herself. Glancing through her open office door, she sat back down and turned toward the window.

After that incredible experience with Tony and Dana, Marissa had spent the week in a kind of a daze. Her workweek was beyond busy, as always, which was a good thing, since otherwise she would have been banging on their door, begging for a repeat experience. When Tony had said she was a natural—born to submit—something had clicked into place inside Marissa, like a door finally unlocking onto a world she'd only dreamed of. She wanted more. More, more, more. But she had no idea where to go to find it.

Tony and Dana hadn't invited her back, though to be fair, they were as busy as she was, if not more so. In her heart of hearts, she knew it probably wasn't a good idea to request a repeat performance. The experience had been more sexual than she had expected, and even if they'd been interested, the concept of a ménage did not appeal.

She thought about joining one of the online BDSM dating sites, but figured they were probably as bogus as the vanilla dating sites, with gamers and posers far outnumbering any real potential partners. The idea of meeting a total stranger to engage in something as intimate as D/s just didn't compute in her brain.

Dana had advised her that the public BDSM clubs could be pretty sleazy. Though there were genuine folks dedicated to the scene, there were even more wannabe bully boys posing as Doms, and needy, lonely girls pretending to be subs just to get a little affection, or at least physical touch. It could be, Dana had warned, a pretty depressing scene.

"Yes. Tony worked it out," Dana replied to her question. "You can come with us tonight if you want, but, uh, there's a catch."

"A catch?" Marissa didn't like the sound of that.

"Well, more of a condition. Membership requirements are pretty strict but Jack Morris, he's the owner of the club, has agreed you can join on a trial basis, provided you undergo a full assessment."

Marissa's heart skipped a beat. "An assessment?" she squeaked.

"Yeah. The way Tony described it, it's a kind of interview and session combined. The trainer needs to assess your submissive potential and decide if you're the kind of person they want joining the club."

Marissa wasn't sure she liked the sound of submitting to whatever some stranger decided for her. In fact, the prospect scared her to death. On the other hand, she really wanted to go back to The Power Exchange, and if this was the only way… "Did you have to do this, uh, assessment when you joined?"

"Me?" Dana replied. "No. But I'm owned. Tony got admittance and I was included as his sub girl. It's unusual for submissives to apply on their own, though it has been known to happen."

"So, give me more details. Would I have to, um, get naked?"

Dana laughed. "Probably. But it won't be in public, if that's what you're worried about. Assessments and training take place in the inner room. I've never even been in there before. It's only for trainers and their clients. Some very intense stuff happens in there, so I've heard. Of course, I'll want a full report."

Marissa bit her lip, her mind veering wildly over the possibilities.

"So?" Dana prodded. "What'll it be? You in?"

"Gosh, I don't know. I mean, I want to, but I'm scared. It's all so new."

"I know. But Tony was right—you're a natural. I frankly have no idea how you got this far in your life without exploring the scene before now." Marissa didn't reply, though since the amazing spanking, she'd been wondering the same thing herself.

"Think of it this way," Dana said. "It's not like you're signing up to be someone's 24/7 sex slave or something. It's just an assessment. If it doesn't feel right, you end the scene, that's all. What are a few hours on a Friday night in the scheme of things? Shit, you went through four years of medical school and three years of residency, for Christ's sake."

Marissa chuckled dryly. "Yeah, talk about torture, but without the eroticism."

"Exactly. Almost as bad as law school, ha ha. But seriously, this should be a piece of cake in comparison. There's no real downside. If what the trainer offers isn't for you, well good, then you've learned something important. But listen, it's totally up to you. You can give this a pass, and you can still come with us again next month as our guest."

That was three weeks away. Marissa could barely wait another second, much less three weeks. And Dana was right—there was no real downside, other than the somewhat terrifying prospect of getting naked in front of a stranger and basically assigning her self-will over to him for a period of time. Yet, even as her mind wavered, her body knew the answer. It was telling her with the thrum of adrenaline racing through her veins, the pulse deep in her sex, the desire vibrating through her bones like a primal drum.

"No," she blurted. "I mean yes. Yes. I want to do it. Please tell them yes for me."

Marissa felt a little foolish as she glanced down at the ridiculously expensive lacy black bra and panty set she'd bought that evening at Victoria's Secret on her way home from work. It wasn't as if she were dressing for a lover, but on the other hand, Dana had advised she would probably be asked to strip, so why not look her best?

She examined her naked form critically in the mirror. Her size C breasts were still firm, her stomach flat, not from dieting but from being too damn busy during the day to eat much. She touched her pubic hair, wondering if she should shave it, as so many women, Dana included, seemed to be doing these days.

She decided that, no, she would leave the neatly trimmed curls as they were. She would feel naked enough as it was, thank you. She sprayed a little *Beyond Paradise* perfume on her throat and wrists, then added a little spritz on her thigh for good measure. She put on the bra and panties and reached for the satin cream-colored chemise-style blouse she'd also bought at Victoria's Secret. She slipped it over her head, reveling in the silky feel of the satin against her skin. It was lower cut than she was used to, but she had to admit she looked good in it.

She grinned nervously at her reflection and reminded herself again this wasn't a date she was preparing for, but an *assessment*. It sounded so formal, so clinical. She wondered who this so-called trainer would be. Would he bark orders at her, like Master Mark had with slave L, and make her do things like scrub floors and lick his boots? God, she hoped not. That had been sexy to watch, but how would she handle it when she was the one on her knees?

A piece of cake, Dana had said. No big deal. And you can always end the scene, Marissa reminded herself. Yes. She could use her new safeword—lemon. She would have to make sure this trainer knew her safeword and understood she had next to no experience. He was a professional. She didn't need to worry. All she had to do was listen and obey. A piece of cake.

Marissa's cell phone buzzed and she glanced at it. *We're a little early. Come down when you're ready,* the text message read. Shit! Dana and Tony were already downstairs. Marissa pulled on her skirt and slipped her bare feet into the higher-than-usual heels she'd only worn a few times before, but which were surprisingly comfortable.

Be right down, she texted back. She ran her fingers through her hair, which had dried naturally into loose waves that fell around her shoulders and framed her face. She had thought about and rejected any jewelry. *Keep it simple,* she told herself. *After all, you're going to be stripping anyway.*

Wrong thought, as it sent her heart once more into overdrive. She reached for her black velvet jacket. A last glance in the mirror, and she grabbed her purse, took a deep breath and murmured, "Piece of cake," as she locked her apartment door.

"Welcome to The Power Exchange."

Marissa looked up to see a fortyish man of medium height with massive arms and a shaved head. He was wearing a black leather vest over a barrel chest, leather pants stretched over muscular, stocky legs. His large nose was crooked, as if it had been broken, perhaps more than once. His eyes were dark and penetrating, and Marissa could feel the power in his gaze.

"Hi," Marissa said. The man held out his hand, which engulfed Marissa's as they shook.

"I'm Jack Morris." His voice matched the rest of him, deep and gravelly. He spoke like someone used to being obeyed. "Tony's told me a lot about you."

Marissa glanced at Tony, who sat with her and Dana at the same table they'd occupied the last time she'd been to the club. Tony lifted his glass in Jack's direction. "All true," he grinned. Smiling at her, he added, "You'll be in excellent hands, Marissa. The trainer who will assess you tonight is regarded as tops in his field—a real pro, and with good reason." He turned back to Jack, adding, "Marissa won't let you down. This one's a keeper, Jack, you'll see."

You'll see? Was Jack going to be her trainer?

Marissa bit her lower lip. Where Tony had been understanding of her fears, and had let her go at her own pace, she strongly doubted Jack would go as easy on her. While the man was certainly compelling, he was also rather formidable, and not what she had visualized. In truth, she'd been harboring a fantasy that she would be trained by someone like the tall, dark and handsome Master Mark from the training videos.

Don't be stupid. This is the chance of a lifetime. Tony and Dana say he's the best. He has to know what he's doing. She realized they were all three staring at her. "If you'll come with me," Jack said, holding out his hand.

Marissa glanced nervously at her friends. Tony was smiling encouragingly at her. Dana put her hand on Marissa's shoulder and gave it an affectionate squeeze. "Good luck," she said softly. "I know you'll do great."

Marissa pushed her chair away from the table. Excitement warred with trepidation inside her as she took Jack's offered hand. She was ready. She wanted this. More than that — she needed this.

Jack stepped to the bar and lifted a panel, gesturing for her to follow him. With a last look at Tony and Dana, Marissa stepped behind the bar. The bartender didn't even glance up as they passed her. They walked through a small kitchen and down a narrow hallway to a set of double doors. Tony turned the knob on one of the doors and pushed it open. He stepped back, ushering Marissa in ahead of him. The room was larger than she had expected and looked something like Tony's playroom, except there were more pieces of equipment, some of which she recognized, some she didn't.

In addition to a St. Andrew's cross, several spanking benches, a whipping post, a medical exam table and a set of stocks, there was an interesting series of rubber strips in one corner strapped to a metal frame. The apparatus was shaped like a huge spider's web, with cuffs and chains dangling from various parts of it. Nearby were two cages, one upright with cuffs attached at the upper and lower corners, and one low and oblong, with newspapers spread on the bottom and what looked like a dog's water bowl set inside it.

Muted lighting was provided by a series of sconces set high along the perimeters of the room. Marissa noticed several racks, some with floggers, some with canes, some with wicked-looking single tail whips of various sizes, the largest a coiled bullwhip that looked like a shiny-skinned, sleeping snake.

Marissa jumped a little when Jack closed the door behind them.

"You can put your things over there." Jack pointed to a small set of cubbyholes, not unlike those found in a kindergarten classroom for book bags and lunchboxes.

"My...things?" Marissa said faintly. She knew she would have to get naked—Dana had warned her. But now that it had come to it...

Jack glanced sharply at her. "Yes. Everything. Strip naked. Oh wait, leave on the heels. You will wait for the trainer on that dais, there." He pointed again, this time toward a raised platform in the center of the room with a set of three wooden steps set along its side.

Did that mean Jack *wasn't* the trainer? Who was? Where were they? She realized Jack was watching her, his bushy eyebrows raised, as if questioning why she was still just standing there.

Don't blow this. Do what he says. Remember, you can always use your safeword.

"My safeword is lemon," she blurted suddenly, and then felt herself blushing.

Jack's lips lifted into a half smile. "That's nice," he said flatly. "Now do what you're told."

Marissa tried to swallow, but somehow her mouth had filled with sawdust. She moved toward the cubbies and reached for the zipper of her skirt with trembling fingers. She realized she had left her velvet jacket over the back of her chair in the outer room. She stepped out of the skirt, folded it and set it into an empty space. With a glance toward Jack, she reached for the hem of her chemise and pulled it over her head. Blowing out a breath, she reached behind herself and undid her pretty new bra. Jack stood with his arms crossed over his massive chest, an implacable expression on his face, his eyes trained on Marissa.

Just do it, she admonished herself. Nudity was the norm at The Power Exchange. Half the people in the outer room were in various stages of undress, and no one batted an eyelash over it. She was being silly and self-conscious. It was just skin. No big deal. She reached for her panties and slid them down her legs, stepping carefully out of them while still balancing in her heels.

She placed the panties on top of her clothing pile and turned to face Jack Morris. His eyes swept over her body, his expression still difficult to read. "Good," he finally said. "Now get up on the dais."

As Marissa moved through the room on rubbery legs she could feel Jack's dark eyes on her. She climbed the small set of stairs and stood on the wooden platform, wondering what to do with her arms. As if reading her mind, Jack said, "Stand at attention, arms up, fingers locked behind your neck, feet planted shoulder-width apart, eyes forward. Don't move until the trainer tells you to move."

Marissa attempted to do as the man had ordered, feeling at once ridiculous and at the same time kind of sexy, naked in nothing but high heels. The position forced her to thrust her breasts forward, and she felt like an object designed to be ogled, which was no doubt the intent of being forced to pose on a raised stage. Rather than feeling humiliated by being put on display, arousal burned its way through her, spreading into her sex and engorging her nipples.

Without another word, Jack turned and left the room by the door through which they had entered, closing it with a small click that seemed to echo in the empty space. Marissa drew in a shuddery breath and released it slowly. Her nose itched suddenly, and she wondered if she dared move out of position in order to scratch it. Keeping her head still, she managed to glance around the room, half expecting to see a camera trained on her. Unless it was hidden, she didn't appear to be observed. Jack had said not to move, but who would know?

The itch was now driving her nuts. She dropped one hand and quickly scratched her nose. Shaking back her hair, she once again assumed the somewhat awkward position, her fingers laced behind her neck. The room was cool, but she could feel the prickle of perspiration beneath her arms, and the dampness of undeniable arousal between her legs.

She was there on a completely voluntary basis, she reminded herself. She could leave at any time. No one was holding her prisoner. This was just an assessment, and Tony had said she was a natural sub. Not that she needed him to tell her. She knew what she was now, or more accurately, she understood now what she had the potential to become. She was being offered a rare and precious opportunity to be assessed by a top trainer.

Marissa heard the sound of a door opening from somewhere behind her. Though she'd been told to keep her eyes straight ahead, Marissa couldn't help turning toward the sound. Her mouth fell open as she took in the figure standing there dressed in a black muscle T-shirt that hugged his broad shoulders and tapered along his body toward a narrow waist and slender hips. He wore black leather pants that looked like they were molded to his long, muscular legs, his feet shod in heavy black boots of the Master Mark variety.

Marissa forgot all about holding her position. Instinctively she tried to cover her naked body. Her heart was thumping like a drum against her bones while her mind struggled to place the man within these surroundings.

His piercing blue eyes moved over her body and settled on her face, and his mouth, like hers, fell open. They stared at one another for several beats of the loudest silence Marissa had ever experienced.

"Dr. Roberts?" he finally said, his voice incredulous.

It was impossible, and yet it was he. No question about it. Her nurse, Cam Wilder, was her trainer. "Holy shit," she exclaimed. "What the hell are you doing here?"

Chapter 5

The shock of seeing Marissa Roberts standing there stark naked, save for those fuck-me high heels, caused something to short circuit in Cam's brain, and he found himself momentarily speechless. He realized now Jack hadn't even told him the subject's name, but only that she was a novice with almost no experience in the scene.

Despite the fact she was trying to cover herself, Marissa's body was even lovelier in real life than the images he'd conjured of her when stroking himself to a quick morning orgasm in the shower. She was blushing sweetly. Her shiny, dark hair cascaded to her shoulders, a deep cleavage created between those luscious breasts by her arms hugging her body.

Cam felt like one of those cartoon characters whose jaw had come unhinged from shock, but his brain sternly ordered him to regain control of the situation. He was the Master; she was the novice trainee. To cede control would be to undermine the entire process. The thing to do was to push on with the assessment. He owed it to Jack, to himself, and to Marissa.

"I could ask you the same thing, sub girl, but we both know the answer. I am a master trainer, and you are here as my subject. You are in the inner room, which means Jack apparently saw something in you worthy of exploration. My job tonight is to assess your submissive potential. As of right now, I see none." He glared at her. "Look at you, out of position, hiding your body from me. The first rule of submission is never hide from your Master—not your feelings, not your fears and most definitely not your body. Back in position, arms behind your head. Now!"

Marissa didn't move. If possible, her face became even redder and she stared at him with flashing eyes, her chin lifting in defiance. If she didn't obey even this most basic command, Cam would end things then and there. He would let Jack know he was not compatible with the subject and hadn't been able to properly assess her as a result. Jack wasn't a forgiving sort of man, Cam knew, and that would be the end of Marissa's chances to join the club.

He would count to three in his head. If she hadn't obeyed by then, he'd walk out. There was no other way.

One...

Two...

He could see the war of emotions moving over her features, but she dropped her arms and then slowly lifted them behind her head, locking her fingers at her neck. Cam could barely admit to himself the vast relief that washed over him at seeing her obey in time. He moved closer.

"I know this is difficult. This is an unusual situation, but we both know you wouldn't be here if you didn't need this. Whatever exists between us outside this room, for right now you are my sub girl and I am your Master. If you find yourself unable to agree at the outset to put everything outside this room aside, we won't be able to move forward, and you might as well get down from there, get your things and go."

She didn't move.

"You want to stay, then? To move forward?" He realized he was holding his breath as he waited for her to answer.

She lifted her chin again, a stubborn look crossing her face. "Yes, Sir." At least someone had coached her to address a Master with respect.

Cam hid his smile, and his relief. "Okay, good. A few ground rules. You will not speak for this hour, except to answer direct questions. When you answer, you will do so as completely as you can. There are no wrong answers. I really do want to get a feel for where you're at each step of the way. If something scares or upsets you, it's okay to ask for permission to speak, and then, once granted, for you to tell me what's bothering you. Though the decision will ultimately be mine, I will listen to you and take your concerns into account."

Cam felt himself settling into his comfort zone, his nervousness and confusion at the bizarre situation dissipating. "To give you an idea of what to expect, first I'm going to conduct a physical examination of your body. After I've assessed your comfort level with being touched, I'm going to put you through a series of exercises designed to determine masochistic reactions, pain tolerance levels, sexual responsiveness, and obedience. You will submit with all the grace you can muster. I will then report to the owner on my findings." He waited a beat while she absorbed all this, and then said, "Are we agreed on this?"

He saw she was trembling slightly, but she nodded and whispered, "Yes, Sir."

Cam climbed the small stairs and stepped onto the dais in front of Marissa. The smell of her perfume, something spicy and floral, mingled with the sharp but not unpleasant tang of fear sweat. Unable to help himself for a moment, he closed his eyes and breathed in her intoxicating scent. Scent had always been a powerful trigger for Cam, and he had to exercise every ounce of self-control not to take the beautiful, trembling woman into his arms and kiss her.

He delivered a rapid, silent lecture to himself that included reminders of professionalism and the limits of this assessment. He'd been attracted to trainees before and he'd managed to keep his tongue in his mouth and his dick in his pants. He would do it now and cut out the teenaged horn dog bullshit.

"I'm going to examine your body now, sub girl," he said, his voice coming out gruffer than he intended. "Your only job is to obey. Understood?"

"Yes, Sir," she replied softly.

He started by walking in a slow circle around her. Stopping behind her, he placed his hands lightly on her shoulders. She jumped a little at his touch, but held her position. He massaged the rigid muscles beneath her skin, allowing a touch of gentleness to enter his tone, now that she was behaving. "Relax, sub girl. Just the fact that you're here means someone saw something valuable in you. Just go with your instincts. Don't try to fight me or yourself as we move through this process."

He continued the massage until he felt the muscles ease, if just a little. Stepping back, he cupped her ass cheeks, which, though small, were full and round, an excellent target for the flogger or the cane.

Or his hand...the intimacy of skin on skin, stroking, then slapping, watching the flesh jiggle and flush to red. He wouldn't stop until she begged him. Erotic pain and lust would intertwine like rope around her senses until she was nothing but raw, submissive desire. Then, and only then, would he slip his fingers into the wet heat between her legs as he pressed against her naked body with his...

Shit. Cam's cock had sprung to rock-hard erection and was straining against the soft leather of his pants. He dropped his hands, closed his eyes briefly and thought about bedpans and patients vomiting into a bowl until his cock got the message and at least partially deflated.

Moving to stand in front of her, he said, "How are your arms? Are you okay staying in that position while I complete the examination?"

Marissa nodded. He lifted his eyebrows until she spoke. "Yes, Sir." He smiled, and she actually smiled back, if somewhat hesitantly. A sudden tenderness swept through him, and impulsively he stroked her cheek, which was indeed just as soft as he'd imagined.

Stepping back, he reached for her breasts, cupping his hands beneath each one and lifting them. She drew in a small breath but didn't resist him in any way. He let them fall and reached for her left nipple. It was dark pink, and it lengthened between his thumb and finger. He tweaked it lightly, pleased at her responsiveness, which manifested as another small, sudden intake of breath and a dilation of her pupils.

His fingers still on her nipple, he looked into her eyes, and she looked back. Were they blue or were they green? He couldn't quite decide. He twisted the nipple, pinching it hard. She gasped and emitted a small cry as she instinctively jerked backward.

He let her nipple go but frowned sternly. "Back in position," he snapped. "I didn't tell you to move."

"It—oh, I..." She pressed her lips together, and then said, "Permission to speak, uh, Sir?"

Jesus Christ, she was fucking adorable. Keeping his expression neutral, Cam nodded. "Go ahead."

"It hurt! That's why I jerked away. I wasn't expecting it."

Cam shook his head, allowing his mouth to curve into a hint of a smile. "It's supposed to hurt, silly girl. You're a sexual masochist, aren't you? Look around you." He waved his arm to indicate all the BDSM apparatus and gear in the room. "Where do you think you are? This is a BDSM dungeon. How am I going to assess your pain tolerance if you can't even submit to a little nipple tweaking? Are you sure you want to be a member of The Power Exchange?"

"No, I mean, yes! I mean, that is, I do want the assessment. I am a sexual...masochist."

She seemed to stumble over the words, and Cam could see this was truly hard for her. What had Jack been thinking, giving him such a complete neophyte to assess? She looked down, but not before he saw tears suddenly pooling in those beautiful eyes. He softened.

"Marissa," he said gently. "It's not too late. You can still back out of this. I'll just explain to Jack that we know each other outside of the scene and—"

"No!" she burst out. "I want to stay. Please. Just give me another chance, okay? I can do this. I know I can. Please, Sir?" She looked up at him, her expression beseeching.

"All right then." He nodded, barely admitting to himself how delighted and thrilled he was she hadn't given up. "Lower your arms and step down from the dais. I'll conduct the physical examination with you lying down. It'll be a little less stressful for you that way."

She nodded gratefully. "Thank you, Sir."

He brought her to the exam table, an old ob/gyn table complete with stirrups. She looked askance at the apparatus. That was supposed to make her more comfortable? She turned to Cam. "You want me to...to lie down on that?"

"Yes," he said, unable to hide his grin. He let her failure to address him correctly slide for the moment. "I do believe lying down for an exam is easier than standing at attention, but if you disagree, we can always go back to the dais—"

"No, no, please. This is fine, Sir," she said unconvincingly, but she didn't move.

Letting a little of his impatience enter his tone, Cam snapped, "Go on. Do as you're told. You know drill. Take off your shoes. Once you're on the table, scoot forward, feet in the stirrups."

He could actually see her girding herself, her shoulders going back, her chin lifting, her hands curling into fists as she moved to the end of the table and turned so her back was to it. She stepped out of her high heels. In bare feet she only came up to Cam's collarbone. She would have to lift her head for a kiss, as he dipped his to meet her.

Idiot. Stop it.

She hesitated another second, but finally put her palms flat on the table and hoisted herself onto it. She slid back against the smooth leather surface and then scooted forward as instructed, placing her feet in the metal stirrups.

Cam moved to stand in front of her, positioning himself between her spread legs. Her body was strong and lean, but still had feminine curves in all the right places. He placed his hands lightly on her legs, and he could still feel the tremble in her limbs. He stroked the soft skin of her inner thighs. "Relax," he soothed. "I am not the enemy, sub girl. I am your Master. You wouldn't be here if you weren't longing to submit. Submit now to my touch and my command. Close your eyes and breathe slowly."

He waited for her eyes to flutter shut. He watched as she dutifully took in a large breath and slowly let it out. "Yes, that's good," he encouraged. "In...and out. Slow and easy. Let all resistance flow out of your body. For this moment, you belong to me."

He moved his hands along her legs, lightly massaging the firm muscles of her shapely calves, and then moving up again, his fingers stroking the sensitive skin where her legs joined her body, meticulously careful not to touch the delicate, sensual folds of her exposed cunt.

Not yet.

He moved around to the side of the table and brought his hands over her stomach and abdomen.

Leaning over her, he cupped each breast, and felt the perk of her nipples hardening against his palms. Though he would have enjoyed lingering there quite a bit longer, he lifted his hands to her slender arms and gently massaged her biceps and triceps before sliding down her forearms. He massaged each hand in turn, pressing his thumbs into her palms and stroking each finger until he felt her relax beneath his touch.

"Lift your arms up over your head." He was pleased when she obeyed without protest and without opening her eyes. He touched her underarms and she startled slightly, but didn't wriggle away. Good — not overly ticklish.

He moved back to stand between her spread knees. Leaning forward once more, he placed his hands around her throat and squeezed lightly. Her eyes flew open, the pupils dilated so wide there was only a ring of blue-green iris rimming them. She gasped, her hands moving toward his. He stopped her with a firm shake of his head. "I didn't tell you to move. You need to trust me, sub girl. You are safe. Keep your arms over your head."

She blew out a shaky breath, but she let her arms fall back into position. He could see that his hands at her throat were a trigger for her, though he surmised by the way she had begun to pant, and the fact that her nipples were hard as pencil erasers, that the trigger was a positive one, even if it was a little scary.

He tightened his fingers at her throat, though he was careful to keep the pressure light as he gauged her reaction. Her lips parted and she began to tremble again, but her eyes were shining and the whimper she emitted sounded sexual to his trained ears.

Why not find out for sure?

Keeping one hand on her throat, he brought the other down between her spread legs. He touched the soft folds of her cunt, which felt damp and hot. Moving his finger carefully between the folds, he sought and found her entrance. The muscles of her cunt seemed to suck his finger inside and then clamp down. She was slippery wet, and as he moved his finger inside her, he applied a little more pressure to her throat. She groaned, her hips arching lewdly upward, which forced his finger deeper into the tight, wet grip of her cunt.

Standing between her legs as he was, his palm was positioned directly over the hard nubbin of her clit, and he pushed and ground against it, knowing full well what he was doing. She actually squealed, her breathy cry sending a jolt of pure lust directly to Cam's cock.

She was shuddering, panting, her hips arched and gyrating as she tried to fuck herself on his hand, and he had never witnessed anything sexier in his life. He wanted her in the worst way. He wanted to rip down his pants and plunge himself into her without mercy or restraint. He wanted to fuck her while keeping his hand tight around her throat, a primordial and powerful display of his dominance and complete control.

Christ, this had never happened to him before, not like this, not with someone he barely knew, and most especially not with someone from the hospital! Someone he would have to face on Monday, who would have to face him.

Jesus, what was he doing?

He pulled both his hands away and stepped back. She lay there panting, her body convulsing as if in aftershock. The skin on her chest, neck and cheeks was mottled pink. Holy shit—she'd orgasmed.

She was sublime. No other word for it.

Without realizing what he was doing, Cam brought his juice-slicked fingers to his nose and inhaled the heady aroma of her musk as he stared down at the beautiful woman. He had to get a grip. He had to regain some semblance of self-control. He was supposedly a master trainer, but he was behaving like a rank amateur.

Marissa opened her eyes and fixed them on his face. He dropped his hand quickly to his side. She bit her lower lip and then said, "Permission to speak, Sir?"

He nodded and cleared his throat. "Yes."

"I'm sorry about that, Sir. I didn't mean to do that. I hope I didn't offend you."

He lifted his eyebrows. "Offend me? In what way?"

She shook her head and looked away. "Never mind, Sir. Nothing."

He had no idea what she was talking about, but rather than slow the momentum any more than it had been, he said simply, "No problem. You're very sexually responsive, and that's a good thing in a submissive. You can get off the table now. It's time to see how well you handle erotic pain."

~*~

Marissa was grateful that Cam didn't make her put the heels back on. She was also grateful for his hand as he led her across the room. Her legs felt wobbly, and her face still burned with embarrassment for having come like that.

The numbness of her shock at discovering that her trainer was her nurse had started to wear off, but it was replaced by a confusing jumble of terror, longing and pure, unmitigated lust. Didn't it just figure that she would fall for a gay guy?

She'd found him attractive at work, but it hadn't bothered her, not really. She wasn't stupid enough to waste her time pining after some gay nurse, and he was easy enough to ignore when wearing his scrubs and sensible shoes.

But seeing him decked out in that muscleman T-shirt and black leather, his usually combed back hair falling into his eyes, his five-o'clock stubble adding a roguish appeal to his features, while she stood naked as a jaybird in front of him—holy cow! She'd nearly fallen down with shock.

And the way he'd stared at her. Yes, he was clearly taken by surprise too, but his eyes had moved over her hungrily, making her feel even more naked than she was, if that made any sense. At the same time, though, it had felt as if he were caressing her with his gaze, as if he *wanted* her. But maybe that was just a talent he'd developed as a trainer—a way to make the submissive feel desired, whether male or female.

She'd told herself she could handle the situation—she wanted to explore this part of herself too much to blow it—and she could have! She was doing okay, that is, until he put his hand on her throat, and his other hand on her cunt.

Something about that big, masculine hand closing around her neck, bringing with it the knowledge that he had complete power over her, erotic and otherwise, had nearly undone her. Her poor clit was throbbing and when he slipped his fingers into her, that was bad enough. But that thing he did with his palm! Oh god, it was amazing. She wanted him to do it again. And again. And again…

Where did a gay man learn to touch a woman like that?

Though she was apprehensive about what came next, she was also excited. *Erotic pain.* Just the words were enough to send a shiver through her loins. Dana was right—how *had* she survived this long without being clued in to her submissive and masochistic needs? And if Cam were anywhere near as capable in the erotic pain department as he was in the giving straight girls orgasms department, she was definitely in for an intense experience.

"I understand from Jack that you've responded well to a bare-handed spanking. Have you ever been flogged or caned? Have you ever been whipped?" Cam's deep, sexy voice pulled Marissa back to the moment.

Her heart jolted into a higher gear at these questions. "No, Sir. None of those things. Not yet."

A smile lifted one corner of his mouth. "Good answer. Not yet. Well, let's remedy that, at least in part. I believe the flogger is the next logical step. I have something new I think would be just right." He moved toward a rack and selected a medium-sized flogger with dozens of black leather tresses dangling from a thick braided handle.

"I think I'll keep you standing for this exercise." He pointed to the polished wooden column that rose from the floor to the ceiling, which Marissa knew from the outer room was called a whipping post. "Hug the post and bring your hands together around it. I'll cuff your wrists so it's easier for you to stay in position. I'll leave your feet free. Since we're at a point in the assessment where it's possible you might need it, what's your safeword?"

Marissa felt a ridiculous but undeniable sense of pride that she had one. "Lemon," she said promptly, adding a belated, "Sir."

"Lemon," Cam repeated. "Okay. Stand at the post. I'll get a new set of cuffs for you." Marissa moved to the whipping post and carefully pressed her bare body against the cool wood. She wrapped her arms around the thick pole and turned her head so her cheek was resting against it.

Cam returned with a set of canvas cuffs with Velcro on either end, a ring of metal dangling from the center of each. He put one around each of her wrists and then clipped them together by the rings. Oddly, instead of making her feel more vulnerable because she was now bound, she found herself easing into a softer place, if that was the word. Somehow the wrist cuffs soothed her, and she wished he would also bind her waist and ankles, but she said nothing.

He moved out of her sight and a moment later she felt his strong body pressed up against hers from behind. He smelled so good! Something woodsy and masculine. She wondered if he had a lover—a partner. Was the guy a sub? Did he cuff him to a whipping post and flog him before making love to him?

Stop it, she ordered herself sternly. *It is what it is.*

"Are you ready, sub girl?" Cam's mouth was so close she could feel his breath tickling her ear.

Though she'd just had a powerful if unexpected orgasm, her perverse cunt, which apparently didn't know the man leaning against her was gay, perked to instant and throbbing attention.

"Yes, Sir," she managed, though in fact she was frightened of the flogger, which had to hurt way more than a mere spanking.

Cam stepped back. "Good. We begin." He appeared once more in front of her and held the handle of the flogger close to her face. "Kiss it," he ordered. "Kiss the flogger as a gesture of your appreciation for what it can give you."

Though this sounded a bit contrived to Marissa, she dutifully touched her lips to the soft, fragrant leather.

He moved again and she could just see him in her peripheral vision. "We'll start light," he said, "and gradually increase the intensity. My goal is to see what you can handle, and how you handle it. Feel free to cry out. It's okay to tell me if it hurts, or to say that you don't think you can take it anymore, and I'll listen to you, though I won't necessarily stop—not until *I* think it's time.

"Regarding your safeword—be very, very careful about using it. It's an absolute last resort, and should only be used if you sincerely believe I'm not getting the message and the action needs to stop immediately. I should tell you, I've never, not once in the six years I've been doing this, had a sub need to use their safeword. I will pay attention to your body and your reactions, and all you really need to do is open your spirit to what I'm giving you. That said, you can use the safeword if you think you have to, but know that all action will cease at that moment, and the session will end. Are we clear?"

"Yes, Sir," Marissa said, now thoroughly terrified at the thought she was going to be taken to the point of crying out and screaming that she couldn't take it anymore. Nonetheless, she was determined to see this through. No way was she going to back down now.

"Okay, then. We begin."

The first strokes were little more than the brush of leather whispering over her skin. It almost tickled. After about ten of these, however, the intensity increased a little, and the leather now lightly smacked her skin, though still nowhere near as hard as Tony's palm had been. This wasn't so bad. She could totally do this!

The flogger moved away from her ass now, landing between her shoulder blades. It stung, but at the same time, it felt good. It felt right. The leather moved down her back to her ass, this time striking harder, so the sting matched that on the thinner skin of her back. Next the flogger shifted to the backs of her thighs.

The first really hard stroke took her by surprise, and Marissa gasped and tensed. "Relax," Cam said at once. "Flow with the pain, not against it."

She had no idea what this meant, but Marissa did her best to relax, in spite of the fact she was naked and tethered to a whipping post, while an incredibly sexy gay Dom smacked her ass with a flogger.

He hit her again, just as hard, and Marissa yelped a little. "Flow with it," she heard him whisper behind her. He struck her again and again, each time a little harder than the last. It hurt, make no mistake, but at the same time her body seemed to crave the pain, just as it had when Tony had spanked her. Or no, even more. She thrilled to the thuddy caress of the flogger as it crashed against her with the force of an ocean's wave.

Yes, her body whispered, *yes, yes, yes.*

And then, without warning, he changed his angle so just the tips of the leather strands made contact with her skin. It stung like hell, and ripped her from the near-trance she had entered. The stinging little tips brushed the sides of her body and it felt like a hive of angry bees swarming over her skin.

"Ow!" she yelled. "Fuck, that hurts!"

"Take it." Something in Cam's tone spoke to something deep inside Marissa's psyche.

The panic that had been rising subsided, and she found that, while the whipping still stung, she could bear it. She could take it.

He resumed the thuddy strokes once more, covering her flesh from thigh to shoulder in a dark, sweet fire of sensation that was nearly as good as, or no, be honest, maybe even better than, sex.

"Oooooo," someone moaned, the word charged with eroticism. Vaguely Marissa was aware she was the one making the sound, but she'd lost the capacity to censor or control her reactions. "Oooooo," she moaned again. There was no more pain, though Cam was flogging her just as hard, if not harder, than before.

Or, no, that wasn't right. It did hurt. But it hurt so *good*. Though she didn't understand it, the erotic pain, the pleasure, the power, the passion of what this man was doing somehow reached past the reserves built up over a lifetime of holding back the most intimate part of herself. It peeled back layers of control, of fear, of longing, of need, reaching to the very core of Marissa's being. "Yes," she whispered, the word a sibilant hiss of pure, raw need. "Yessssssssss..."

Her head felt heavy and she let it fall back. Her bound hands around the post were the only thing that kept her from sliding into a puddle on the floor. She was no longer Marissa Roberts, MD, or Marissa Roberts the woman, or even Marissa Roberts, the sub girl. She was just sensation. Pure, perfect sensation, her spirit rising from her body as the leather kissed and stroked her skin with what she could only define as love.

When she opened her eyes, she was confused to find herself on the ground. She was leaning back against someone, whose strong, masculine arms were wrapped around her from behind. As she came more fully to herself, she realized it was Cam holding her. She must have somehow passed out or something.

Whatever had happened, she was engulfed in a deeply satisfying sense of utter well-being. Though still disoriented, she leaned back her head and smiled up at the gorgeous sexy man who was holding her.

Defenses completely lowered, she blurted, "Wow, that was fucking amazing. No offense, but it really sucks that you're gay."

Chapter 6

"I'm sorry, what?" Cam was sitting behind Marissa on the floor near the cross, his arms around her. He had been rocking her gently as she returned to planet earth, drifting in a pleasant fantasy that he wasn't her trainer, but rather her lover—the lover who would soon carry her to bed and make love to her.

Her words smashed through his reverie like a fist to the jaw, and he actually whipped his head back from the impact. Marissa twisted to face him, extricating herself from his arms in the process. "Oh!" she exclaimed "Sir. I should have said Sir. I didn't ask permission to speak. I forgot. I—"

"No, no," Cam interjected. "That's okay, Marissa. The assessment, the scene—it's over. It's okay. This is called aftercare. Where I help you come down from the high of the experience. No more Master or Sir required."

She looked relieved. "Oh, okay, then. Phew."

Cam smiled, but he wasn't about to drop the subject. "So, I need clarification here. You think I'm gay?"

She bit her lower lip, her eyes sliding away from his. "I'm sorry," she said. "I hope that wasn't rude to say. It just kind of slipped out."

Cam couldn't help it. He started to laugh. He supposed he shouldn't have been surprised. Marissa knew him first as a nurse, and he'd heard the whispers and seen the looks of some of the staff when he passed by.

She met his eyes, crossed her arms over her breasts and frowned. "What? What's funny?"

He shook his head. "Forgive me." He was still grinning. "I hate to burst your bubble, but I'm straight as an arrow."

Her expression moved to one of confusion. "Wait, what? You mean you're...you're not gay?" she stammered. Color was washing prettily over her cheeks and throat.

It took every ounce of self-control for Cam not to gather her into his arms. "No, I'm not. What made you think I was? Surely not just because I'm a nurse?"

"No, not at all," she said with such conviction he wondered if she, if not lying, was perhaps hedging the truth a bit.

He didn't let her off the hook. "Okay, so then...what?"

Again she looked away. "Oh, well, the other nurses were saying, I mean...Janice saw... Oh god, I'm really confused right now."

Cam relented. "Hey, I'm just busting your chops." He pushed himself to his feet and headed toward the wall hooks where the clean robes were hung. He grabbed one and returned to her. As he placed it around her shoulders, he said, "So, I'm all ears. What juicy gossip did Janice have to spread this time?"

Marissa offered a rueful smile. "So, you're already on to her, huh? You're right. I should have considered the source. Usually I know better. She swore she saw you going into a gay sex shop in the Village."

Cam slapped his forehead. "Ah, now I remember. I did see Janice down in the Village the other day. What she actually saw was me heading into C&C's." Marissa looked blank, and Cam elaborated. "It's a BDSM gear shop. I suppose, in Janice's defense, not that she deserves any, the mannequin in the window at C&C's is a male dressed in BDSM leathers and chains, a ball gag over his mouth. She obviously drew her own conclusions."

Marissa started to laugh, a full-throated, open laugh that filled Cam with an irrational joy. He started to laugh too. Still chuckling, he leaned toward her and extended his hand. She took it, allowing him to help her up.

They regarded each other for a long moment, each growing serious again. Cam's lips tingled with the need to feel the press of her mouth against his, but he held himself in check.

Marissa tied the sash of the robe around her slender waist. "So," she said, pushing her hair from her face and tucking it behind her small, pretty ears. "Tell me the truth. How did I do tonight? Did I pass the audition?"

"You did, Marissa," Cam said sincerely. "I can honestly and without reservation recommend you to Jack as a provisional member of the club."

As he said it, he silently marveled at how little anyone knew about the people they worked with. Dr. Roberts, with her brisk, no-nonsense manner on the job, was secretly a passionate, sensual masochist with incredible potential as a submissive. And here she'd been right in his backyard, so to speak, and he'd had no idea.

"Provisional?" she countered.

Cam smiled. "Yeah. Jack is super cautious about admittance. He had a few problems with some guys a while back that nearly got the place shut down, so he's very careful about who he accepts. Three months probation, and you can join as a full-fledged member."

There was a sharp rap at the door. Cam glanced at his watch. "Oh, shit," he said. "I have a client booked for the next hour. That's my five-minute warning. I'll just talk to Jack real quick and let him know you're in."

"Oh. You have a client? Now?" Marissa looked crestfallen, which made Cam smile again. He realized he'd been smiling so much in the last few minutes that his cheeks actually ached.

Taking a chance, he said, "Listen, could you maybe wait for me? It's a light night. I only have one half-hour session after this one coming up. I'd love to take you out for coffee or a glass of wine or something." Suddenly he realized the assumption he'd made, and he added quickly, "I mean, uh, that is, if you came alone."

"I came with my friends, Tony and Dana. Do you know them?"

Cam nodded. "I know who they are, but I don't know them well." He offered an apologetic shrug. "I don't get a chance to spend much time in the outer room. I mostly work with clients and potential members back here. So" —he assumed a casual tone— "Tony and Dana are just...friends?" He'd learned in the scene not to make assumptions about the nature of D/s relationships, and ménages, especially those consisting of a Dom and two subs, were not all that unusual.

Marissa smiled. "Just friends. Really Dana is my friend. Tony's her husband. But he's the one that got me this, uh, assessment."

"So, would they be cool if you came with them, but left with me? More to the point, would you be cool with it?"

Her smile widened and she ducked her head in a coquettish way that had nothing to do with Marissa Roberts, MD and everything to do with a sexy, flirtatious sub girl. "Yes, Sir. I'd be very cool with it."

~*~

Dana and Tony were still sitting where she'd left them when Marissa returned to the outer room. Dana's hair was a bit disheveled, her mascara a little smeared, which led Marissa to think they'd been doing some scening of their own during her absence.

"Well," Dana said eagerly, as Tony stood and pulled out a chair for Marissa. "How did it go? Tell us everything!"

Marissa sat, offering a nod of thanks to Tony. "It went great," she said, unable to stop the wide smile that spread over her face.

Dana was regarding her expectantly. "Come on, details, girlfriend! I've never even seen the inner room. I want a full description of everything that happened, from the second you entered the room until you came out here with that big ass smile on your face."

Tony sipped his wine as he regarded his wife with an indulgent smile.

Where to start? Marissa had already decided she didn't plan to share the fact that she and Cam worked together. She had a sense that would be violating his privacy. Nor did she plan to divulge her deeply personal, visceral response not only to what he'd done, but to the man himself. It was all still so new and precious—she wanted to have time alone to digest, dissect and savor every moment.

"Let's see," she said, composing her thoughts. "The place wasn't all that different from your playroom, except more equipment and more gear." She went on to describe the basics of what the assessment entailed, leaving out their conversation during the aftercare, or the fact that Cam had pulled a powerful climax from her.

"It sounds amazing," Dana breathed, hanging on to every word. "So what happens now?"

"Cam, er, the trainer, is going to talk to Jack. He says he's going to recommend me for provisional membership."

"Well, that's great!" Dana enthused. "Oh, Marissa, I'm so proud of you!"

"Well done," Tony echoed. "Congratulations."

As if on cue, Jack Morris suddenly appeared beside their table. "Excuse me," he said, staring down at Marissa. "If I might have a word with you in private?"

Though she knew the news was good, something about his tone and the way he seemed to look past her eyes into her most secret thoughts was disconcerting. Marissa swallowed and nodded. As she pushed back her chair, Jack said to the others, "If you'll excuse us for a moment."

"Of course." Tony nodded, waving them away with his glass.

Marissa followed Jack to the bar, where they both sat on stools at the far end, away from anyone else.

Jack swiveled on his stool to face her. His voice was deep, and power seemed to radiate from his pores. "The trainer was quite positive in his assessment, Marissa. I'm pleased to offer you a provisional membership, assuming the terms of our membership agreement meet with your approval."

He pulled a piece of paper that was folded lengthwise from his back pocket and spread it on the bar in front of Marissa. "You can read that at your convenience, and if you are agreed, just sign and return it to me."

"Thank you, Sir." The "Sir" had just popped out without any premeditation. Jack exuded an authority that seemed to require the appellation. "I really appreciate it."

Jack stood. Staring into her eyes, he stroked her cheek with a single, large finger. Though she wasn't sexually attracted to Jack, his touch sent a shiver through her, and she had a sudden nearly overwhelming desire to fall to her knees in front of him.

Fortunately, he broke the spell. Dropping his hand, he said brusquely, "Enjoy the rest of your evening, Marissa. I look forward to seeing you again." She stared after him as he strode away.

Dana appeared beside her a moment later. "What did he say? What did he say? Are you in?"

Marissa held up the piece of paper he'd given her. "This is the provisional membership agreement. I just have to sign it, and yes, I'm in." She grinned suddenly at the prospect.

They returned to the table. Marissa scanned the document quickly. It was basically a confidentiality agreement, with Marissa promising to keep everything that went on at the club strictly private, along with some rules about proper conduct, exchange of bodily fluids and management's responsibility or lack thereof for any injuries suffered during play. It also outlined a fee schedule that seemed quite reasonable to Marissa.

Tony asked to see the document, and pulled out some reading glasses to peruse it. After a moment, he pronounced that he saw no legal reasons for her not to sign. He produced a pen and held it out to her.

Marissa took the pen and signed on the dotted line at the bottom of the page, a whole swarm of butterflies suddenly swooping inside her. "It's official then," Dana said, watching her. "You're now a sister sub in the BDSM community. Welcome to the most exciting and supportive group in the world." She stood and leaned over Marissa, giving her a big hug. Sitting back down, she added, "Now, we just need to find you a Master."

Marissa's smile widened into a grin. "Well," she said, "about that…"

"What?" Dana demanded. "What about that?" Her eyes widened. "Hold on. You aren't saying Jack...? Jack doesn't even like—"

"No, no," Marissa interrupted with a laugh. "Not Jack. Cam. The trainer." As Dana's eyes widened, Marissa hurriedly amended, "I'm not saying he's going to be my Master or anything. But when the trainer is done with his sessions in about an hour or so, we're going to, I mean, he's invited me out for a drink."

Dana regarded her for a few seconds, her face splitting into a widening grin. "Marissa Roberts, get out of town! That dude has a rep as untouchable. Never scenes in the outer room. You spend forty-five minutes with him and whammo, he's taking you on a date?"

"You saw how responsive Marissa was in our playroom," Tony interjected. "Are you really so surprised?"

"Surprised?" Dana shook her head. "No, not surprised. Just pleased as punch. Way to go, Marissa, honey."

Marissa shook her head and gave an exasperated laugh. "It's not a date. Why do I feel like you two are marrying me off? We're just going for a coffee or something. We actually know each other from the outside."

Oops. She hadn't meant to say that. Oh well, the cat was out of the bag, but she'd make sure and leave it at that.

Both Tony and Dana looked surprised. "Really? But that's amazing. Who is he? Do you work with him?" Dana demanded. Tony put his hand on Dana's arm and gave a small shake of his head.

Marissa picked up the membership agreement. "Confidentiality," she reminded Dana. "I shouldn't even have said that much."

Dana nodded. "You're right. I'm sorry. Forget I asked." She leaned close to Marissa's ear and said in a stage whisper, "You can tell me later."

~*~

The waitress brought them each an espresso in a tiny porcelain cup and set a plate of baklava between them. Cam had found himself on autopilot several times during his sessions, and had to force himself to forget Marissa long enough to do his clients justice. Now he was free to focus entirely on the lovely woman who sat across from him.

She lifted a piece of the sticky honey pastry and took a bite, her eyes fluttering shut in appreciation. Cam grinned, pleased she seemed to like his choice of location and dessert. "It's delicious, right? I love this place, and they're open until three a.m., which is great when you work nights like I do at the club."

"I'm still trying to get my head around all this. There's a whole world out there I never even dreamed of, to tell you the truth. This is all so new."

"Tell me a little about your experience in the scene," Cam said. "I know you've had no formal training, but obviously you've been involved in some way in D/s, right?"

Marissa shook her head. "Not really. Until very recently, I was what my friend referred to as sub-curious."

"Sub-curious." Cam smiled. "I like that." He took a bite of his baklava as he waited for her to continue.

"Yeah." Marissa smiled. She had an adorable dimple in her left cheek, and another in her chin. "I mean, I've had these kinds of feelings—submissive feelings I guess you'd say, pretty much all my adult life, but I didn't really know what to call them, and I certainly didn't act on them. Not until recently, that is." She told him about Dana, and the events that led to the assessment.

"That's a pretty incredible story, Marissa. I mean, based on your reactions during the assessment I was sure you'd had at least some experience beyond what you're telling me. Your responses were so powerful— so passionate. I've worked with a lot of subs in my time, and for some it takes years to fly the way you did. Hell, some never do. Your ability to let go—to trust—it's quite remarkable."

Marissa ducked her head and smiled shyly. "It's because of you," she said softly. "You made me feel..." She paused, seeming to look for the word. "Safe."

"Thank you," Cam said, her words warming him to his toes. "That means a lot to me. Trust is the foundation of D/s."

"It's the foundation of a lot of things," Marissa said, looking up. "There's something about you, Cam. I guess it's what makes you such a good nurse, too. In the short time you've been at the hospital, you're already making quite a reputation for yourself, did you know that? You make people feel safe there too, both staff and patients alike. They know they can trust you. It's a gift."

Cam couldn't stop the wide smile that Marissa's words brought to his face. "Thank you," he said again. But her mention of the hospital brought him back to one of the things he wanted to talk to her about. "About the hospital," he said. "Obviously we work together, and I hope it's equally obvious that I want to see more of you. Is there going to be a problem, a conflict in that regard?"

Marissa pursed her lips, as if weighing what she wanted to say. Cam ached to kiss those sweet pouting lips, but held himself in check, taking a bite of baklava instead. Finally she said, "More of me, huh? I think you've seen just about all of me there is!" She smiled, though a rosy blush bloomed on her cheeks.

Cam laughed and put his hand over hers, pleased when she didn't pull it away. "I want to see more, to know more. Much, much more. And not as a trainer hired to give an assessment. But as a man with a woman."

Marissa's eyes were bright and Cam was pretty sure he didn't imagine the sudden shudder that moved through her frame at his words, or the nearly imperceptible sigh. After a moment, she cleared her throat and offered a small embarrassed laugh. Assuming the professional tone Cam was used to at the hospital, she continued, "Normally I make it a personal policy to keep work and personal life separate. I mean, it's just easier that way, don't you agree?"

Cam nodded, as he did in fact share the philosophy. "Then there's the complication of me being a nurse and you a doctor," he offered, saving her the trouble of stating the obvious.

He was pleased when Marissa shrugged this away. "Oh, that's not an issue. Not for me." She regarded him with those lovely blue-green eyes. "Is that a problem for you?"

Cam shook his head. "Not in the slightest. Though it might be an issue for some others — staff consorting and all that."

"Want to know what I think?" Marissa said, lifting her chin.

"I do," Cam said, fighting the urge to reach across the table and kiss her. "Tell me."

"I think we're both mature adults who have made an unusual connection outside the workplace."

"Unusual, yes," Cam agreed, smiling.

"I think we're both professional enough to behave on the job as if nothing has changed. I don't know about you, but I'd just as soon not offer myself as sacrificial grist for the Janices of this world to run through their gossip mill. So if it works for you, I'd like to see more of you, too. At work, we're just Dr. Roberts and Nurse Wilder. What we do on our own time..." She let the sentence trail away.

"Is our own business," Cam supplied. He lifted his coffee cup aloft. "To new beginnings," he said.

Marissa lifted her cup and lightly touched it to his. "To new beginnings," she replied.

Chapter 7

They stood in front of her apartment building and watched the cab pull away from the curb. Cam had said he'd take the subway to his place once he'd seen her safely inside. Marissa didn't want the evening to end, though at the same time she was conflicted. Should she invite Cam up to her apartment? Was that tantamount to admitting she wanted him to stay the night? Did she?

She'd been lobbing the idea back and forth in her mind as they rode from the café to her apartment. In the backseat, Cam had put his arm around her shoulders, and she leaned into him, marveling at the perfect fit. She was still high from the whole inner room experience, not to mention how easy Cam had been to talk to afterward. But did that mean they should just tumble into bed? Did he expect her to make the first move? Or, as the Dom in the relationship—*Relationship? Slow down, girl!*—would he be appalled by her forwardness?

Marissa had made a rule for herself several years back that worked well for her—no sex on the first date. She'd succumbed too many times to the persistence of guys she barely knew, guys who were thinking with their cocks and just wanted to get what they could while the getting was good. More often than not, she regretted her decision afterward, and couldn't wait to get the near-stranger she'd somehow thought she was attracted to out of her bed and out of her life.

Loneliness, too much to drink, the desire to be held, the need to just let go—none of those were good enough reasons to fall into bed with a guy she'd just met.

But she hadn't just met Cam. They worked together. She'd been able to observe him on the unit for the past several weeks. He was a genuine person—a kind and compassionate nurse. He wasn't a serial killer or some horny, desperate type who would ejaculate as soon as his cock touched a woman's bare thigh.

Then there was the session in the inner room. The way he'd touched her—so sensual, yet so dominant. Her every instinct had thrilled to him, even when she'd thought he was gay. She wanted to see him naked. She wanted to run her hands over his muscular body. She wanted to feel his cock inside her, his comforting, masculine weight on top of her. She wanted to make him ache for her, as she already did for him. He was twenty-nine, she was thirty-two. They weren't kids. What was she waiting for?

Cam shoved his hands into his pockets. There was a light wind, and his hair blew into his eyes. His lips were parted as if he were about to speak. She wanted to kiss him. She wanted him to kiss her.

Fuck her self-imposed rules.

"Want to come up?" she said before she could stop herself.

Cam spoke at the same moment. It took a second for her brain to unscramble what he'd said at the same time as she. "I'll say goodnight, then, Marissa."

"Oh!" she said, feeling the heat rise in her face.

Cam looked a little embarrassed too, but he smiled. "It's better if we say goodnight, I think." His tone was kind, which somehow compounded her humiliation. "You've got a lot to process. The session—everything you experienced—sometimes it's easy to confuse desire for what someone offers with desire for the person himself." He paused a beat, as if expecting Marissa to say something. She wasn't about to help him in his rejection. She stared at him. He smiled and reached to stroke her cheek, and in spite of herself, Marissa leaned into his touch.

"I want you, Marissa. Please don't think I don't. I know if I came up with you now, I wouldn't be able to keep my hands off you. You're beautiful, bright, passionate, submissive—everything I want in a woman. That's why I don't want to fuck it up by moving too fast with you. It's late. I want you to get some sleep, take a little time to put things into perspective. Maybe we could go for breakfast in the morning? See where we stand in the light of day?"

Marissa knew he was right. In fact she did need some time to process the amazing events of the evening. What she was feeling might be no more than a rush of infatuation. Maybe she was just so excited about her own submissive discoveries that she was confusing that with desire for the man who had bound her, flogged her, made her heart pound and her entire body vibrate with longing...

Cam was watching her again in that way he had, his full attention on her as if nothing else existed in the world. She forced a smile and shrugged. "Sure. Yeah. Breakfast sounds good." Standing on tiptoe, she kissed his cheek and then turned abruptly away, fumbling for her keys and turning the lock.

She got the door open, and Cam was just behind her, opening it farther for her, the perfect gentleman. "Marissa." He put his hands on her shoulders and spun her gently toward him. He took her in his arms and lightly kissed her mouth, then let her go. They had exchanged cell phone numbers earlier in the evening, and he said, "Call me in the morning? Promise?"

Marissa nodded, feeling a little better. He was just being sensible. It was good that someone was, since she was ready to shuck her clothing right there in the lobby and throw herself at him. "Yeah. In the morning. Get home safe."

She turned and walked toward the elevator bank, forbidding herself to look back. She pressed the button. The ancient elevator lurched noisily from somewhere overhead and began its descent. When the door opened, she started to step inside, but suddenly strong hands gripped her shoulders and she was whirled to face Cam, who pulled her once more into his arms.

"Who am I kidding?" he said, as he buried his face in her hair. "I can't leave you. If I have to wait until tomorrow to kiss you, I'm afraid my body will spontaneously combust. Can I come up? Please, beautiful Marissa, can I make love to you?"

Marissa laughed and pulled him into the waiting elevator car. "I thought you'd never ask."

~*~

Cam managed to wait until Marissa got the door to her apartment open, but that was about all he could manage. She barely flicked on the light and shut the door when he grabbed her shoulders and pressed her against the wall, holding her in place with his mouth on hers while his hands roamed feverishly over her body.

Marissa was panting against him. He slipped his fingers under the silky top and the lace of her bra. Cam grasped her erect nipples and gave each one a twist. Her breathy gasp went straight to his cock, which was already hard as steel.

"I want you," he murmured, taking one hand from her breast and slipping it beneath her skirt. He slid his fingers between her legs, pulling at her damp panties and pressing a finger into the clutch of her tight cunt. Marissa groaned, the sound primal and raw.

Cam reached for the hem of her skirt and flipped it upward to her waist. She gasped but made no move to resist him. He grabbed the lacy panties with the intention of pulling them down, but the force of his grip ripped the flimsy lace, so he just pulled the torn panties from her body and tossed them away. He forced her legs wider with his knee and continued to stroke her now-bared cunt, sliding his fingers in and out of the slippery wetness. He could smell her desire, ripe and feminine, and his cock strained in his pants.

Her knees started to give way, and he placed a steadying hand on her shoulder to hold her in place. Her head was tilted to the side, her eyes closed, her mouth slack. He ground his palm against her clit while continuing to stroke her from the inside out. Marissa's moans shifted to grunting little cries.

Unable to hold back a moment longer, Cam reached for his fly and yanked it down. With one hand still at her sex, he managed to pull down his pants and underwear far enough for his purposes. Gripping her by the hips, he guided his throbbing cock into the folds of her cunt and pressed his way carefully inside, using every ounce of control not to simply ram his way into her.

Placing his hands beneath her ass, he lifted her as he buried himself inside her, and this time he was the one who groaned, the sound wrenched from somewhere deep inside him. Marissa locked her legs around his hips, pulling him deeper into her wet, perfect heat. Her arms came around his neck and her lips found his.

They kissed as he lifted and lowered her on his shaft. The pleasure was nearly unbearable. He was nothing but lust—pure, dark, tumultuous lust. Marissa was trembling against him, emitting little staccato cries, her tight cunt spasming against his shaft. Cam wanted it to last forever, but knew he was hanging on by a thread.

"Oh god," Marissa cried suddenly. "Oh, god, oh god, oh god!" She jerked in his arms, her movements snapping that slender thread. Cam exploded inside her, the blood roaring in his ears, his heart convulsing in his chest, his entire body melting from the blasting fire of his orgasm.

Finally Cam sank slowly to the floor, Marissa still wrapped around him. He leaned back with her in his arms, his cock still buried inside her. He stretched out his legs and she moved with him until they were lying flat, he on his back, she on top of him, her head nestled against his neck.

He must have drifted off for a minute or two, because when he opened his eyes, Marissa was beside him, peering into his eyes, a very feminine, satisfied little smile on her pretty face. "Hi," she said softly.

Cam lifted himself onto one elbow. "Hi there. Nice place you have here."

"Wait'll you see the bedroom," she quipped with a grin.

Cam chuckled and Marissa started to laugh. Cam laughed too, happiness nearly levitating him from the floor. He pulled Marissa into his arms, his cock hardening against her thigh. "I don't think you're going to get too much sleep tonight," he growled into her ear.

"Sleep is overrated," she murmured. Then she kissed him.

~*~

Marissa's grandmother had loved musicals and was always playing them on her old-fashioned vinyl record player when she had Marissa and her little sister, Kristen, over for the weekend when they were children. One of her grandmother's favorites, and therefore by extension one of Marissa's, was the soundtrack to *The King and I*. Marissa's favorite song on the record had always been *Hello Young Lovers*. The lyrics had been playing in her head all that morning, and she'd even found herself humming while typing up some notes at a terminal in the nurses' station after rounds: *I know how it feels to have wings on your heels and to fly through the street in a trance. You fly down the street on the chance that you'll meet and you meet – not really by chance.*

That had been happening all morning with her and Cam. She'd seen more of him on the unit that Monday after their incredible weekend than in the weeks he'd been on staff. Every time they saw each other, it was hard to resist exchanging a secret smile, or brushing his hand when he handed her a chart, or standing a little too close when they consulted on a patient.

It was surely only a matter of time before the rest of the staff, especially the ever-observant Janice, realized there was something going on between them. While they had agreed there was no reason to hide the fact they were seeing each other, neither did Marissa want to come across to her staff as a lovesick teenager. Hopefully she would be better able to hide her feelings once they got more used to handling themselves in public, and once the relationship wasn't so blindingly shiny and new.

Was it possible to fall in love over a single weekend?

Probably not, Marissa's rational, sensible mind informed her. But her heart and her body were telling her otherwise. Cam and she had barely left her apartment the entire weekend, and for the first time in years and years, Marissa's pussy was actually sore from use, and she'd had more orgasms than she could count. She was glad she'd continued taking birth control pills after her last breakup six months prior, since no way did she want to have anything, even a thin membrane of latex, come between her and this amazing man. And sex was the least of it. Or not the least of it, but made a thousand times more intense by the delicious erotic overlay of BDSM.

Cam had spanked her—not the way Tony had, while she was strapped to a cross, his wife watching nearby. That had been exciting in its way, but nothing compared to the intensity she'd experienced while lying naked over Cam's muscular thighs, her hands bound at the wrists with old stockings, his cock hard against her belly as he turned her ass a blistering cherry red, and then flipped her over to fuck her to yet another in a series of blindingly intense orgasms.

When they were too tired for sex, they talked. They talked about everything, from their respective childhoods, their interest in medicine, to how they lost their virginity. Cam had lost his during his senior year of high school in the backseat of his car after the prom—his girlfriend had been so scared Cam's cock had wilted several times while attempting to penetrate. Marissa had held out until freshmen year of college. The junior jock she'd chosen had turned out to be much better at playing football than at making love to a woman.

She'd felt comfortable sharing her earliest sexual fantasies, which had always included a strong man "having his way with her" but had only fairly recently taken a more specific masochistic and submissive turn. She'd felt validated by Cam's understanding and encouragement, and excited by the promises he made to take her as far as she was ready to go into the heady and thrilling world of D/s.

As she moved through her workday, Marissa had to force herself to focus. She owed it to her patients to give them her full and undivided attention, and after a while, she somehow managed to tuck Cam and the amazing weekend into the back of her mind.

Then she would see him again, just his back as he was walking away, or his profile as he leaned over the nurses' station counter, and her entire body would leap to life, every nerve ending thrumming with need.

Would the day never end?

~*~

"Wow, this is really nice." Marissa turned slowly in the small living room of Cam's house—the right side of a duplex located in Queens. "You probably have twice as much space here as I do in my apartment."

Cam nodded. "No way could I swing even a studio in Manhattan, but out here there are still some affordable neighborhoods, and it's right off the subway line. Wait'll I show you upstairs."

"The bedroom?" Marissa said in a teasing voice. "Is that where you're taking me?"

"Even better." Cam waggled his eyebrows and grinned.

Marissa followed him up the stairs to the second floor. Cam led her past two open doors—one the master bedroom, its bed neatly made, the other an office with a desk and bookshelves overflowing with books. "Where are you taking me?"

"To my own personal inner room," Cam said with a sexy smile. He stopped in front of a door at the end of the hallway and turned to her, his expression now serious. He put his hands on her shoulders and looked deeply into her eyes. "Marissa, you've told me over the course of the week that you're ready for more. You want a more total slave experience. Is that still true?"

In the week they'd been together, Cam had stayed over at her place most nights, and the BDSM play, while intense and exciting, hadn't progressed much past spankings, light bondage and some breath play. Marissa was ready for more, and Cam had promised that today they would begin to delve deeper into her masochistic impulses and desires. Something swooped in Marissa's gut at his words, and her nipples perked inside her bra. "Yes, Sir," she said throatily.

Cam nodded. "I'm going to take you into my dungeon. Once you cross the threshold, you are no longer Marissa. You are slave M, and you are my property to do with as I will. Do you think you're ready for that?"

Marissa stared at her new lover. Property! The very idea was anathema to an independent, strong-willed doctor. But Cam wasn't talking to her as a professional. He was speaking to the only recently acknowledged yearning Marissa had discovered deep inside — the need to give herself completely to another person — to submit not only with her body, but with her heart and soul.

She swallowed hard and nodded. "Yes, Sir. I'm ready."

"A slave never enters my dungeon dressed in street clothing. Sometimes I will have you dress in ways that please me. For now, you will strip and leave your clothing, all of it, at the bottom of the stairs." He pulled open the door, revealing a flight of steep, narrow stairs. He looked at her, waiting.

Though Cam had seen her naked a dozen times over the past week, she felt suddenly shy, maybe because he was still fully clothed, or maybe because something had changed in his demeanor. He was once again the trainer from the inner room, and she the trembling novice.

Yet she knew there was really no decision. Or more accurately, that she'd already made it. She pulled her shirt over her head and then opened her jeans as she stepped out of her sandals. He watched her with smoldering eyes as she reached back to unclasp her bra and then slipped off her panties. She folded the clothes and placed them on the bottom stair. She stood, twisting her hands nervously behind her back.

Cam held out his hand and she unclasped her hands and placed one in his. He led her up to the finished attic. Instead of the usual boxes and suitcases, there was a St. Andrew's cross, a spanking bench, a kind of chain and pulley mechanism hanging from the ceiling, a rack filled with whips, floggers, canes and paddles and, in the corner, a camp cot with a pillow and a neatly folded stack of blankets on top of it. The floor had been covered with a wood laminate that gave the appearance of hardwood. In another corner stood a small sink and a toilet, partially hidden by a partition.

Small, high windows on two of the four walls let the afternoon sunlight into the space. Beneath one of the windows there was an old end table with several dozen candles on it, some of them partially burnt down. Marissa's imagination immediately shifted into overdrive as she thought about the women Cam must have brought here over the years.

"Stand at attention, there." Cam pointed to a thick square of carpet set in the center of the room beneath the pulley and chains that hung from the ceiling. Marissa moved into position, her heart thumping. Cam came up to her and stood close. She could smell the scent of his sandalwood aftershave as he leaned down to kiss her lips. She started to reach for him, but he stepped back with a shake of his head.

"I didn't tell you to move. You will not make assumptions, slave M. Nor will you take liberties. You will do as you are told, and nothing else. Am I clear?"

"Yes, Sir," Marissa breathed.

He reached for her breasts, capturing her nipples between his thumbs and forefingers and twisting them, lightly at first, and then harder so she winced. In spite of the pain, or no, because of it, she felt a gush of desire throb through her sex, and a small moan escaped her lips.

He let go of her nipples and reached for her throat with one hand, the other sliding down over her mons. Gripping her pubic hair, he tugged lightly at it, while his other hand tightened at her throat. "To be a submissive sex slave is to be completely accessible to your Master. Nothing shielded, nothing hidden. If you are sincere in your wish to belong to me, I will require that you are shaved smooth at all times."

He wasn't asking her, she realized. He was informing her this was a condition. Though only a few weeks before Marissa would have refused outright, she found herself excited by the prospect, even eager. "Yes, Sir. I want that. I want to be fully accessible to my Master."

"Are you ready now, slave M?"

"Yes, Sir," she answered without hesitation, surprising herself with the strength of her conviction.

"Excellent. I have everything we need under the sink. You will lie back on a stool and remain perfectly still while I groom you."

He brought a high stool with a wide, round seat and set it down. He went to the cot and returned carrying a towel, which he draped over the stool. He directed Marissa to perch on it, legs spread, feet anchored on the rungs.

Cam went to the sink in the corner of the room and turned on the water. Reaching into the cabinet beneath it, he pulled out various items, including a large plastic bowl, which he filled with water and a squirt of liquid soap. He returned to her with the water bowl, a second smaller bowl, a disposable razor, a pair of scissors and a small can of shaving cream.

"Reach behind you and grip the back legs of the stool," Cam said.

Marissa reached back as directed, feeling at once lewd and sexy with her breasts thrust forward by the arch of her back, and her pussy on display. She tried to stay very still as the sharp scissors snipped around her privates. Cam worked quickly but carefully, dropping tufts of pubic hair into the empty bowl. When he was done, Cam lifted a washcloth out of the water bowl, wrung it out and placed it over her mons. He rubbed the cloth gently over her, lingering at her clit, which had already swollen and hardened while he was trimming her. After a few moments, he dropped the washcloth back into the bowl.

He shook the can of shaving cream and squirted a small amount onto his palm. He spread it with his fingers, lingering teasingly at her labia until she began to pant with desire. Ignoring her, he took the disposable razor and pulled away its plastic wrapper. He worked with sure, careful strokes, moving the fingers of his left hand in the wake of the razor until he was satisfied. When he was done, he took the washcloth again from the sudsy, warm water, wrung it into the bowl and then gently washed away any remaining shaving cream.

He stepped back to look her over. "Beautiful," he said, the admiration clear in his tone and in his expression. "You're like a work of art." He met her eyes and smiled. "You may sit upright. I want to show you the full effect."

He moved quickly toward the back wall, returning with a full-length mirror, which he placed in front of Marissa. She stared at the image of her denuded sex, fascinated and surprised. She had expected something along the lines of a plucked chicken, and instead saw the petals and folds of an exotic flower in varying shades of pink, darkening to red in her lust.

Cam crouched in front of her and placed a hand on either thigh, forcing her legs wider apart. He leaned toward her sex and touched her hooded clit with the tip of his tongue. Marissa blew out a shuddery breath as he drew his tongue in a long, smooth line between her labia.

Cam lifted his head to look at her face. "Don't come. You do *not* have permission to come. Understood?"

Marissa nodded, and whispered, "Yes, Sir."

His warm, wet tongue felt like heaven as it glided over and between her labia and teased in a swirling circle around her clit. His kisses felt different—more intense, more sensitive—without the cover of pubic hair. Marissa knew at this rate she wasn't going to last long. When he pressed a single finger into her wetness, Marissa cried out involuntarily, "Oh god! Fuck me. Please."

"Shh. No talking," Cam admonished, before ducking back to lick and suckle her.

Marissa felt the uncontrollable rise of an orgasm as Cam relentlessly licked and fingered her. "I can't," she gasped. "I'm going to, please, oh, Sir. I can't help, oh…"

An orgasm thundered over and through her and she began to shake on the stool. Cam gripped her thighs harder, never letting up, though he had to be aware she was coming. She moaned, the sound deep and guttural in her throat, and then rising to a high, piercing wail she was powerless to suppress.

When he finally pulled back, she fell back against the stool and would have toppled off it if Cam hadn't been there to pull her into his arms. Still cradling her, he sank to the carpet with her in his lap. "Naughty, naughty girl," he said into her ear. He chuckled. "If you were properly trained, I would have to whip you for that transgression, slave girl. But I'll cut you some slack, since this is your first time in my dungeon."

Marissa, her breath returning somewhat to normal, looked up at Cam. "I'm sorry," she began in a rush. "I didn't mean to. It was just so intense. I was trying not to but—"

Cam silenced her with a finger to her lips. "Shh, it's okay. I don't need to hear any excuses. You did what you did. There's no getting around that. And while I'm not going to whip you, you are going to be punished."

"Punished?" Marissa whispered, her breath catching in her throat.

"Perhaps punished is too strong a word in this instance," Cam said. "Corrected might be the better term." He pushed her gently from his lap and got to his feet. "I'm thinking some nice hot wax melted onto that smooth, disobedient cunt of yours will be a good reminder in the future of what happens to slave girls who come without permission. Have you ever had hot wax dropped on your labia?"

Marissa felt suddenly faint, and she reached instinctively to cover herself with her hands. "On my labia?" she echoed.

"Answer the question."

"No. No, Sir. Isn't that dangerous?"

Cam shook his head. "Not with the right candles. It will scald a bit—leave you a little tender perhaps, but no lasting harm. As I say, a good reminder. We'll use the spanking bench for this. You will lie on your back, ass on the edge of the bench, feet planted firmly on the ground on either side, legs spread. I'll put a cushion under your ass so you can offer your cunt more easily."

Again, he wasn't asking—he was instructing, and Marissa found herself getting to her feet and walking toward the bench. She waited while he brought a towel and a cushion from the cot. He placed the cushion on the bench and draped the towel over it. "Go on," he said, pointing to the bench. Marissa lay down, her pussy still gently throbbing from the orgasm, her heart fluttering wildly.

Cam left her and returned a moment later with a fat red candle on a small china plate, a box of matches beside it. He placed this on the floor beside the bench and knelt next to her. He reached for her face and gently stroked her cheek as he gazed into her eyes. "Do you trust me, slave M?"

"Yes, Sir," Marissa replied without hesitation.

"Good. I promise never to give you reason to doubt that trust." He picked up a small bottle and squirted something into his hand. "This oil will make the wax removal easier afterward." He rubbed the oil over her mons and labia, his touch sending electric currents of desire through her.

"Control yourself," he said, though he was smiling. He lit the candle and held it over her groin. "You will keep your legs spread and your cunt offered up to me. You will not move out of position. You may cry out, and if you are in true distress, you may use your safeword. But I think you can handle this. In fact, I know you can. This particular wax is made for this kind of play. It will hurt, but it's not dangerous. Remember, this is just a correction as we begin to work on orgasm control."

He held the candle over her spread sex and Marissa tensed. Though she believed him that it was safe, she clenched her hands into fists as she waited with anxious anticipation. She squealed as the first hot drop landed on her smooth mons, more out of fear than actual pain. When wax landed on the tender folds of her inner labia, her cry of pain was real. But she could do this. She could and she would. For Master Cam. For herself. She arched her hips upward in silent offering.

"You make me proud," Cam said softly. There followed a steady stream of splashing hot liquid until her mons and labia were covered in the cooling red wax.

"Thank me for the correction, slave," Cam said when he was done.

"Thank you, Sir," Marissa replied, surprised to realize how much she meant it.

Using a small metal comb, more oil and a wet cloth, Cam easily removed the dried wax, leaving Marissa's smooth cunt tender, but otherwise none the worse for wear. Finally he reached for her hands and helped her to her feet.

"I think that's enough for a while. Let's go downstairs. I have something I want to show you." He led her down to the second floor, retrieving the pile of her clothing and tucking it under his arm as they moved down the hall. He stopped at his bedroom and said, "What I want to show you is in here."

He led her to the bed and pushed her gently down. Quickly pulling off his clothing, he climbed naked onto the bed beside her.

"What did you want to show me?" Marissa giggled, snuggling against him.

"How much I love you," Cam replied, pulling her into his arms.

Chapter 8

One night as they lay in bed together after lovemaking, Cam lifted himself onto an elbow. "Hey, I almost forgot to tell you—Jack and his partner, Jessie, are having a piercing ceremony to cement their bond as Master and slave. Jack has invited Dorian Martin, a master piercer and body artist, to do the honors. I thought you might like to observe. Dana and Tony will be there. What do you think? Would you like to go?"

"A piercing ceremony?" Marissa tensed at the thought, at the same time experiencing a sudden, unexpected thrill of longing.

Cam nodded and smiled. "A ritualistic piercing can be a symbol of ownership—of submission. Who knows"—he shrugged—"we might want to look into it for ourselves when you're ready." He pulled her into his arms, whispering into her ear, "A lovely little gold ring on your labia—a sweet, private reminder that you're cherished and owned."

"Me? My labia?" Marissa squeaked, pulling back to look into her Dom's face.

Cam laughed gently, his beautiful blue eyes crinkling at the corners. "Only if and when you're ready, darling. That's never something I would demand of you. It would have to be something you asked of me."

"Oh." Conflicting feelings of relief and dismay moved through Marissa. Sometimes she just wanted to be told what to do. Isn't that what Masters were supposed to do? Even as she thought this, she knew Cam's approach was the correct one. She understood Cam had no desire to run roughshod over his submissive, taking her power from her, but rather he continually sought to engage her, while always respecting her physically, intellectually and psychologically.

Marissa had come a long way since fantasizing about the kind of submission Master Mark demanded on the online BDSM site. What Cam offered was real, and while it required Marissa to respond with courage and grace, it was worth all the effort she put into it, and then some.

For now she decided to focus on the invitation itself. It was gratifying to realize she was becoming an accepted member of the BDSM community, one invited to events such as this. She leaned again into Cam, who wrapped his arms around her. "I'd love to come," she said, resting her check against his warm chest. "I look forward to meeting Jessie."

The next morning at the gym, Dana and Marissa agreed they would meet after work to go shopping for new outfits for the occasion. "I'll help you pick just the right thing for a night at Jack's place," Dana said with a grin.

Thinking back to the elaborate and extremely revealing outfits Dana liked to wear to the club,

Marissa laughed. "Oh, I just bet you will. I get the final say, though, agreed?"

They went to Dana's favorite BDSM boutique in the Village. The small space was filled with racks of leather bustiers, corsets and dresses. Boots and high heels lined the floor around the perimeter of the room, and BDSM gear and paraphernalia hung from hooks along the walls, hefty price tags dangling from their handles.

Dana selected leather bras with the cups cut out, crotchless leather pants, and miniskirts so short they would barely cover a person's hips, much less the rest of them, each time announcing the item would be perfect for Marissa. Marissa chuckled and shook her head at each outrageous suggestion.

"Come on, Marissa," Dana urged. "You're not a newbie anymore. Quit with all the modesty crap, will ya? Oooh!" she interrupted herself, moving toward a pair of thigh-high boots with six-inch heels. "These are perfect!"

"If it's all right with you, I think I'll choose a few items on my own," Marissa said with a laugh. "You just focus on you."

Reluctantly Dana agreed, after extracting a promise from Marissa to "step outside the box".

Marissa finally settled on her outfit—a long black velvet skirt that hugged her hips, with slits on either side to mid-thigh, and matching black velvet open-toed high heels. She paired the skirt with a low cut black leather corset with thick satin sashes crisscrossing in front and back. The salesperson pulled them so tight Marissa could barely breathe, but she had to admit as she regarded herself in the full-length three-way mirror that the effect was stunning.

"Wow!" Dana enthused when she saw Marissa. "You're right. You *can* do your own shopping. I was a fool to ever doubt it," she quipped with a grin. She had chosen a black leather miniskirt and the thigh-high boots she'd had her eye on, along with a sheer white silk blouse beneath which her bare, perfect breasts proudly jutted.

Marissa had to admit, she hadn't had this much fun shopping for clothing in years—if ever. She couldn't wait to wear her sexy new outfit. She felt like a caterpillar just coming out of its cocoon, ready and eager to spread her wings.

Tuesday night found Marissa jumpy with excitement and nervous energy. As they rode the subway from Cam's home in Queens to Jack's Chelsea apartment, Marissa looked around at the other passengers, wondering what they'd think if they had any idea that this handsome man beside her in his unassuming white knit shirt, faded jeans and sneakers would soon transform into a sexy Master, his lean, muscular body clad in a black leather vest and leather pants soft and smooth as a second skin.

How marvelous to think this man—this kind, compassionate nurse, this sexy, thrilling Dom—loved her, Marissa! Another bit of lyric from one of her grandmother's favorite songs drifted into her mind, this one from *Westside Story*—*and I pity any girl who isn't me tonight.*

The doorman at Jack's apartment building seemed to know Cam. He nodded and smiled as he pulled the door open for them. "You can go on up, sir," he said, doffing his uniform cap. When they arrived at Jack's fifth floor apartment, a slender man in his early thirties opened the door. He had a shock of red hair and narrow, merry green eyes over a small, freckled nose. He was shirtless, his lower half clad in loose white linen pants held up by a drawstring at the waist. His feet were bare. A thin collar of dark green leather with a gold padlock dangling from an O-ring at its center circled his neck.

The man stepped back to welcome them in and, after exchanging a hug with the man, Cam turned to Marissa. "Marissa, allow me to present Jesse O'Brien, Jack's partner and sub."

Not Jessie, a woman.

Jesse. A man.

Marissa took a second to readjust her brain as she realized her error. She hoped her initial puzzlement hadn't shown on her face. She held out her hand. "Very pleased to meet you, Jesse."

Jesse took her hand in his. "Likewise, I'm sure." He spoke in a soft, Southern drawl. Everything about him was a contrast to the dark, powerful presence that was Jack, but as Marissa well knew, opposites often attracted. "Master Jack's just making a pitcher of Sangria," Jesse continued, shutting the front door behind them. "Dana and Tony haven't arrived yet."

Jesse glanced at the large duffel over Cam's shoulder. "Did y'all want to change? You know where to go, Cam. We'll be in the living room. Sangria good for you both? Or would you rather have iced tea?"

"Sangria's perfect," Cam said. He glanced at Marissa. "You?"

"For me too." She nodded, thinking a little wine might help ease the nervous fluttering in her belly.

They walked through a nicely appointed living room with fine leather furniture, large wooden bookshelves lined with books and framed photos, and striking black and white photographs of city landscapes on the walls. The whole apartment was suffused with the delicious aroma of baking bread.

Cam ushered Marissa into a large windowless dressing room, though instead of clothing and shoes, the walls were lined with enough BDSM gear to stock a small store, along with racks containing a large assortment of whips, floggers, crops and paddles. Two of the four walls were entirely covered in mirrors. There was an empty clothes rack with a few hangers dangling from it.

Cam dropped the duffel on the carpet. Reaching for Marissa, he gripped her gently by the shoulders and looked into her eyes. As Marissa stared up at him, all the chatter and hubbub of the workweek was quieted in her head. The tension she hadn't even realized she'd been carrying slid from her like a discarded jacket. Her lips parted and her breathing slowed as she focused on her Master.

She could feel his power, and her entire body thrilled to its call. "Sub girl," he said in a clear, low voice.

"Sir," she replied, held willingly captive by his penetrating gaze.

"There are rules in Master Jack's house. You will obey the rules as if they were mine."

"Yes, Sir," Marissa agreed, transfixed.

"In Master Jack's house, subs do not speak unless spoken to, except to ask permission to speak. They don't sit on furniture, or use utensils. Any Master's word given to you tonight is an instant command to be obeyed without hesitation or question. Does this suit you, slave girl?"

Marissa felt suddenly dizzy, as if she'd already had the offered wine. A flush moved over her skin and her nipples ached with longing. "Yes, Sir," she whispered.

Cam released her and turned toward the duffel. She stood frozen for several moments as she watched him take out their things and lay them on the carpet. He stood and pulled his shirt over his head. Marissa's mouth actually watered at the sight of his muscular chest and tapering waist. When he slid out of his jeans, she had to catch herself to keep from moaning out loud.

Stripping quickly, she pulled on black stockings with the pretty lace at the thigh, the only underwear that would be permitted tonight. She slid on the velvet skirt and picked up the corset.

She turned again to Cam, who was lacing the crotch of his sexy leather pants. "I'll need your help to get this on, Sir."

"I'm tempted to have you wear only the stockings and heels."

Marissa pressed her lips together to keep from making a decidedly un-submissive retort. Mutely she held out the bustier.

Cam grinned. "Okay, okay," he relented.

Together they fitted the corset around her midriff. Standing behind her, Cam pulled the satin stays into position. As they tightened, Marissa's waist was cinched, her breasts plumped together to create deep cleavage. She couldn't help but stare at herself in the mirror. A part of her brain still had trouble reconciling the sexy, curvaceous woman who stared back at her with her deeply ingrained persona as the no-nonsense Dr. Roberts.

"You are breathtaking," Cam said from behind her. He pushed her gently but firmly against one of the mirrored walls so her back was to him, her cheek resting on the smooth glass.

His body was hard behind her, his erection poking like a fist into her lower back. Marissa's entire being throbbed with desire. She wanted Cam to fuck her then and there, without tenderness, without mercy.

There was a knock on the door. "Hey, quit monopolizing the changing room. There are people waiting, you know." Marissa recognized Tony's voice. The knob turned and Cam stepped back from Marissa, who swallowed her groan of dismay.

They exchanged quick hugs with Dana and Tony, and returned to the living room. Jack was standing with a man Marissa hadn't yet met. Before introducing him, Jack and Cam exchanged greetings and a hug. Jack nodded toward Marissa, his dark eyes moving over her like fingers. Marissa felt herself flushing beneath his penetrating gaze, but managed to keep her arms at her sides.

"Welcome to our home, Marissa. You look lovely," he said, finally releasing her from his stare. "Dorian" — Jack turned to the tall, thin African-American man with large, dark eyes and friendly smile — "allow me to present Cam's sub girl, Marissa. She's new to the scene."

Dorian extended his hand, and Marissa took it, feeling shy but ridiculously pleased to be referred to publically as Cam's sub girl. "A pleasure, Marissa,"

Dorian said in a smooth tenor, his long fingers cool and strong around hers. He wore a white button-down shirt open at the throat to reveal his smooth chest. The shirt was tucked into leather pants the color of toffee.

Jesse appeared from the kitchen with a tray containing wine glasses and a glass pitcher of Sangria with slices of orange and lemon floating on top. He set the tray on the coffee table beside a platter of cheese and crackers. Dana and Tony entered the room a moment later. Dana was stunning in her short skirt, see-through blouse and thigh-high boots and Tony looked suave in a black silk shirt and black linen pants over designer Italian loafers.

Cam, Jack, Dorian and Tony sat down—Jack and Dorian on chairs, Cam and Tony on opposite couches. Large flat pillows were strategically placed around the sitting area. Dana lowered herself carefully in her short skirt beside Tony and laid her head sweetly on her husband's knee. Jesse sat cross-legged beside Jack, his face suffused with happiness as Jack stroked his shoulders and back.

Marissa lowered herself to her knees beside Cam. He placed his hand on the back of her neck and his touch sent an electric jolt of desire through her. He leaned close and whispered, "You belong to me, slave girl."

Jack poured the drinks and handed out the glasses. Marissa drank the chilled, fruity wine, relaxing as the alcohol's warmth suffused her body.

The four seated men exchanged small talk about mutual friends, favored piercing techniques, the latest BDSM gear and various other topics while Dana, Jesse and Marissa stayed quiet and sipped their wine.

It was an exercise in restraint for Marissa not to chime in with an observation or opinion. At one point Dana smiled and winked at her, as if to say, *Look at us, a physician and an attorney, barely dressed in our leather and satin, kneeling at the feet of our Masters!* The odd thing was, Marissa found she didn't really mind. Or no, to be honest, she found the situation rather thrilling. She felt vibrant and alive, and excited about the coming ceremony.

Jack and Jesse served a delicious meal of grilled rib eye steaks with sautéed mushrooms, mixed salad with balsamic vinaigrette and thick slabs of homemade bread slathered with melted butter. It was a strange experience to kneel on a cushion on the floor beside Cam and let him feed her, though Marissa had to admit there was a certain eroticism to it she hadn't expected. Dana and Jesse seemed completely at ease beside their Masters, which made it easier for Marissa to accept.

When the meal was over, Jack led them all into a carpeted room that contained a medical exam table complete with stirrups. A thick, white towel covered the padded leather. There was an antique library table beside it, the small lamp on it providing the only light in the room. Beside the lamp were dozens of shrink-wrapped needles set neatly in rows, along with clamps, gauze pads, cleaning solutions and other items reminiscent of a surgeon's operating room. A pile of additional clean towels was folded in a laundry basket nearby. Three folding chairs faced the setup, a flat silk cushion placed beside each chair. Narrow, high shelves were set against the walls, the surface of each covered by tall, fat candles set in brass holders.

Jesse and Dana moved together toward one of the candle shelves. Jesse lit two long, narrow tapers and handed one to Dana. They began to light the candles, moving quickly from table to table until the room was illuminated with the warm, flickering glow of candlelight.

Dorian, meanwhile, stood conferring softly with Jack. Tony was already seated, and Cam sat down beside him, beckoning Marissa to join him. She knelt on a cushion next to her lover. He bent down and kissed the top of her head. "I love you," he whispered.

It was on the tip of Marissa's tongue to respond, until she remembered Cam's warning in the dressing room. She would honor the house rules, and so she only smiled.

Her attention was diverted to the shiny needle Dorian was unwrapping from its protective plastic. She could imagine its sharp prick against her skin. While the thought sent a shiver of fear through her body, at the same time she couldn't deny the fizz of excitement skimming along her skin like tiny bubbles.

The candles all lit, Dana returned to kneel next to Tony. She smiled warmly at Marissa, who smiled back.

Jesse went to stand beside Jack in front of the exam table, their backs to the room. Dorian stood in front of them like an officiating minister. Jack reached into his pocket and pulled out a small velvet jewelry box, which he handed to Dorian. Dorian opened the box and set it on the library table.

Turning back to Jack and Jesse, Dorian placed a hand on either man's shoulder. "We are gathered here this evening," he began, "to witness Jesse's offering to his Master, Jack, a ceremonial display of his submission. Jesse willingly undergoes this piercing as a testament of his love and obedience. Jack accepts this offer and bestows the gift of his ring, a permanent and daily reminder for Jesse of Jack's love and mastery."

He took a step back and gestured toward the exam table. Jesse unlaced the string that held up his pants and, without a trace of self-consciousness, let them puddle at his feet. He was completely naked underneath, and shaved smooth as a baby. Jack and Dorian helped him settle onto the exam table and place his feet into the stirrups.

Unbidden, the image of herself up there on that table, naked, legs spread wide, filled Marissa's mind, and her body tensed as if waiting for the sharp bite of the needle's point to pierce her flesh. She shuddered and then felt Cam's warm, comforting hand on her back. She leaned into him, relaxing beneath his touch.

Dorian put on a pair of disposable latex gloves, selected a needle and moved to stand between Jesse's legs. He wiped the underside of Jesse's now erect cock with a cleansing pad and touched the point of the needle to the chosen site.

"You will feel a pinch," he said. "Just breathe in and let it out. Stay centered on what matters, which is your love and devotion for your Master." Jesse nodded. "Count to three," Dorian continued. Jack was standing beside Jesse, holding one of his hands and looking down at him with a tender expression.

"One...two...three." Dorian moved his hands. Marissa couldn't really see just exactly what he was doing, but she could hear Jesse's sudden intake of breath. Dorian reached for the small stainless steel Prince Albert ring, wiped it with a sterilized pad and slid it into place on Jesse's cock.

"Done!" Dorian said, smiling broadly at Jack, who grinned back. "It's perfect."

As if they'd all been holding their collective breath, everyone in the room seemed to sigh at once. Then they all laughed and clapped their hands in approval as Jesse sat up on the table, his face beaming with happiness and pride.

As Jack helped his partner from the table, Marissa noticed Dana tugging urgently at Tony's sleeve. "Please, Sir. May I speak?"

Tony turned to Dana with a smile. "Of course, darling. What is it?"

"I decided. I'm ready," she said eagerly as she jumped up from the cushion. "Please, Sir. Please, Master Tony. I'm ready for my piercing."

Marissa gaped at Dana with astonishment. She hadn't said a word about being pierced. What the hell? As if feeling her gaze, Dana turned to Marissa with a small shrug. *I wasn't sure,* she mouthed silently. *Now I am.*

Tony and Dana went to stand where Jack and Jesse had been. Dorian stripped away the towel on which Jesse had lain and smoothed a fresh one in its place.

Marissa looked up at Cam. With a smile, he took her hand into his. *Do you want this for me?* Marissa silently telegraphed to her lover. She recalled what he'd said when he first told her about the piercing ceremony: *That's never something I would demand of you. It would have to be something you asked of me.*

Do I want it?

Marissa tried to concentrate on Dorian's words, but her mind kept veering to another scenario, one involving Cam and her. She was lying on that exam table, legs spread, her hand in Cam's as Dorian slipped the needle through her labia. Was it really so simple? She only had to ask?

As if he were listening to her thoughts, Cam squeezed Marissa's hand, though his eyes remained fixed on the couple in the front of the room.

Marissa watched as Dana removed her blouse, her small, high breasts standing proud on her chest. Marissa was surprised when Dana let Tony help her onto the table while still dressed in her boots and skirt. How would she spread her legs in that tight skirt? Marissa turned to Cam, confused. He mouthed the word *nipples*.

Marissa turned back, trying to process this new information and adjust her expectations accordingly. Tony handed Dorian a slightly larger box than the one Jack had produced. Dorian opened the box and Marissa saw what looked like the gleam of diamond in the candlelight as he set it on the library table.

Dorian put on a fresh pair of gloves. He squeezed some antiseptic liquid onto a gauze pad and wiped both of Dana's erect nipples with the cleaning solution. He and Tony quietly discussed the precise placement of the jewelry, and then Dorian gripped one of Dana's nipples between thumb and forefinger, pulling it taut.

"Breathe," Dorian intoned, the needle poised for insertion. "Take the pain for your Master. Embrace the pain for yourself. One...two...three."

Dana yelped, the sound high and shrill, and Marissa gasped, her own nipples aching with sympathy. Dorian reached for one of the nipple rings, wiped it with the sterilized pad and slid it into place using the tiny plastic sheath still threaded through Dana's nipple.

"Perfect," Dorian pronounced as he daubed away a bit of blood. He reached quickly for the second needle and pulled her other nipple taut, while Tony murmured something close to Dana's ear as he stroked her face.

"One...two...three."

Again Dana cried out. Dorian worked quickly, and soon had the second hoop in place. Dana sat up. She was laughing, her cheeks flushed, her eyes shining. "Oh my god! I did it! I did it! Tony, I did it!" Dana touched the gold rings hanging from her nipples, a small, round diamond set into each ring.

Again there was laughter and applause. Jack and Jesse joined the couple as Tony and Dana embraced. Cam and Marissa stood as well. Marissa could barely focus, emotions skittering and slamming into each other in her brain, the overriding one of which was, she realized with a shock, a longing so intense it took her breath away.

I want that. I want it too.

She looked at Cam, at once surprised, but not really, to find he was staring at her, rather than at the revelry in front of them. She had never been with a man like Cam, someone who seemed to intuit her emotions and her needs almost before she did. She felt *known*, and the realization warmed her down to her toes.

"Are you ready, sub girl?" Cam said in a low voice. "Is it your turn?"

"Yes," Marissa whispered. And then louder, as she sank to her knees in front of her Master, "Yes, please, Sir."

Cam reached down and held out his hands. Marissa took them, allowing him to pull her to her feet. "But," she said with dismay, "we don't have a ring."

Cam's smile broadened into a grin as he slipped his hand into his pants pocket. "Actually, we do." He pulled out a clear plastic bag, holding it on his palm so Marissa could see. Inside was a tiny gold ring with a small gold ball holding it closed. "I bought it when Jack first invited us, just in case."

"If I could have your attention," Cam addressed the room, which immediately quieted. "My sub girl and I wish to share in the piercing ceremony tonight." He held out the ring. "Marissa has agreed to accept this gift of ownership."

Yay! Dana mouthed as Marissa and Cam approached the front of the room. Marissa smiled, the crazy butterfly flutter in her belly quieting a little at her friend's sweet and enthusiastic show of support. They stood together in front of Dorian. Cam took Marissa's hand as Dorian intoned, "Marissa, do you give this gift of submission freely to your Master?"

"I do," Marissa said, turning to look at Cam, whose radiant smile was like warm sun on her skin.

"And you, Cam, do you accept Marissa's loving offer of devotion and her willingness to wear your ring?"

"I do."

"Please disrobe and take your place on the table," Dorian said to Marissa. Pleased to note her hands weren't even trembling, she unzipped her skirt and let it fall to the carpet. She stepped out of her high heels and let Cam help her onto the table. She placed her feet into the stirrups, nervous but determined.

Cam stepped beside her and took one of her hands in his. "I'm so proud of you, Marissa," he said softly.

Marissa kept her eyes on Cam's face as Dorian gently cleaned the spot he and Cam agreed on for the piercing on her right outer labia. She looked into his deep blue eyes as she felt the tug of Dorian's gloved fingers. "Breathe," Dorian commanded. "Take in the peace and serenity that is submission. One...two...three."

There was a sharp pinch and then a sudden burning sensation.

And then it was over.

A rush of endorphins hurtled through Marissa's bloodstream, and she laughed with sheer joy. And then everyone was laughing with her. Cam pulled her from the table into his strong arms and whirled her in a circle before setting her down. Dorian was saying something about aftercare, but Marissa didn't hear a word. She knew Cam would take care of her.

In a happy daze, she pulled her long skirt back into place while Tony and Jack moved around the room blowing out all the candles, and Dorian packed his gear into a leather case.

Cam, with his arm around her, led Marissa back into the living room along with the others. Marissa sank happily to the silk cushion beside Cam. She accepted the large snifter of brandy that Jack handed her. Once they all had their glasses, Jack lifted his and the others followed suit.

"A toast to our cherished submissives," he boomed, "who daily fill our lives with love and happiness."

"I second that emotion!" Tony cried.

"I third it!" Cam added. They all laughed, and drank their brandy, and Marissa felt happier than she ever had in her life.

Chapter 9

"Psst."

Marissa looked up at the sound and saw Cam standing just inside the walk-in linen closet. He crooked a finger, beckoning her to him. With a quick glance to left and right, Marissa hurried over to the closet. Cam pulled her inside and closed the door behind her. He drew her into a quick embrace.

"I haven't seen you in days," he murmured, nuzzling his mouth against her ear.

"Weeks," she replied.

"Years," he amended.

They both laughed and stepped apart. "You ready for tonight, slave M?" Cam watched the transformation as he said those words. Marissa was extremely responsive to language, and every time he used words that triggered a submissive response, something in her expression would soften and bloom.

"I hope so, Sir," she said softly, her eyes shining.

Cam had secured the inner room for a full two hours tonight just for them. Though they'd been to the outer room a number of times together, this would be Marissa's first return to the inner room since her assessment. Cam planned to use the time to create a training video for their private use. Since the piercing ceremony, Marissa had been increasingly receptive to deeper and deeper levels of erotic submission, but she was sometimes her own worst enemy, letting her fear of failure get in the way of her development.

Cam had found training videos to be a useful tool when training clients. Though this was his first time taping someone with whom he was personally involved, he saw no reason why the tool wouldn't be equally as effective. They would watch the video together, without the overlay of tension and passion that invariably accompanied a scene. It was a way to target areas for improvement, and highlight resistance or hesitation subs didn't always realize were in play during the heat of the moment.

Tony and Dana would be joining them in the inner room, not only as witnesses, but to assist with the recording. "You'll be fantastic," Cam had assured Marissa when she expressed some anxiety. "Sometimes it's hard for me to believe you've only been active in the scene for such a short time. You truly are a natural."

Now Cam took a step back, assessing Dr. Roberts in her white lab coat, her hair pulled back into a barrette, a stethoscope hanging around her neck. "Just think," he added with a grin, "if anyone in this place had any idea of the fiery, passionate woman lurking just beneath that no-nonsense doctor image you present to the world, it would blow their minds."

"Or the leather-clad, whip-wielding Dom disguised as the hard-working, dedicated nurse," Marissa retorted with a saucy grin.

"Gay nurse, you mean," Cam added with a laugh. When Marissa wasn't exciting him down to his bones, or making his heart melt with her sweetness, she was making him laugh. He'd never thought he could have it all, but with Marissa it seemed that he had found "the one" at last.

He pulled her once more into his arms, this time kissing her on the lips. For a moment, he forgot where he was and slipped his tongue into her mouth as he pressed his body against hers. She moaned softly against him and kissed him back, her arms coming up around his neck.

The door opened suddenly and they instinctively pulled apart. "Oh!" Marissa said, her cheeks coloring as she looked toward the intruder. Cam turned his head to see Janice standing there, a load of dirty linen in her arms.

Janice's painted-on eyebrows rose up so high they were hidden by her hair-sprayed bangs. "Well!" she huffed. "Excuse *me*!"

"So, I'll get those lab results for you right away, Dr. Roberts," Cam said briskly, unable to completely wipe away his grin.

"Thank you, Nurse," Marissa said faintly.

Cam brushed past the gawking Janice, turning back to wink at Marissa. At least those rumors of his sexual orientation would finally be put to rest, he thought with a grin as he strode down the hall.

~*~

Though she'd only been there once before, Marissa couldn't help the sense of proprietary pride she felt as she watched Dana and Tony taking in the setup, aware this was Dana's first time to see the inner room. "This is fantastic," Dana breathed, her expression rapturous. Turning to Tony, she said, "I want that, and that, and that," as she pointed to various pieces of BDSM equipment and gear.

Cam directed the couple to sit on folding chairs he'd set up in the center of the room. While he selected gear for the evening's play, Tony put the camera bag he'd brought along on the floor beside him and bent down to unzip it. He pulled out a tripod and erected it, and then took out a small camcorder, which he screwed into place on top of the tripod.

Though Marissa had understood and even agreed in theory with the concept of a training video, she felt jittery as she watched Tony setting up. It was one thing to scene with her friends, or to share in the piercing ceremony, with everyone equally involved and invested in the process. Tonight Marissa would be the focus and the center of everyone's attention. All eyes, including the camera's, would be on her and her alone.

Marissa looked over at Cam as he approached, his arms filled with gear, a smile on his face. He set down the things on the edge of the platform and put his arm comfortably around her shoulder. "You still okay with the recording?" he asked. Somehow he always seemed to know just exactly what was troubling her. It was as if they were connected from the inside out.

"Remember," Cam added as he pulled her close, "this is just for us. We can delete it once we're done. But if you're not comfortable with it, we'll bag it, okay? It's not a requirement."

"I am a little nervous about it," Marissa admitted, "but I do see the value of watching yourself after the fact. And since it's just for us…"

"Of course," Cam agreed. He let her go and stepped back. He looked fantastic in his leathers, a beautiful, heavy flogger dangling from one hand.

"Are you ready, slave M?" he said in a louder voice, one meant for Dana and Tony to hear.

Marissa glanced in the direction of their friends. Tony was adjusting the camcorder, but Dana was looking at her, and she gave a quick encouraging smile and a thumbs-up. If it wasn't for Dana, Marissa would never have gained the understanding, or found the nerve, to move forward in this amazing submissive exploration. She felt empowered by Dana's support and grateful for her and Tony's friendship. She was glad they were there as witnesses as she continued in her submissive journey.

Turning back to Cam, she nodded and said in a clear voice, "Yes, Sir. I'm ready."

"We've invited our friends to witness a work in progress," Cam said, his voice rich and deep. "Tonight I'm going to ask Master Tony for input, as part of your ongoing training in submission." He turned to Tony. "We've been working on endurance positions, caning, mid-level bondage, flogging and single tails. Is there something you would like to see demonstrated tonight?"

"What about anal?" Tony said.

Marissa's stomach clenched, but she kept her eyes on her Master.

Cam lifted an eyebrow, looking thoughtful. "We've talked about that some," he said slowly. "We really haven't explored anal yet, but it's definitely on the list."

On the list maybe, but way, way down there! Marissa wanted to blurt, but she managed to hold her tongue. Marissa had confided to Cam that, while she'd engaged in anal sex from time to time in her life, it was not her favorite activity. "I'm really shy about my butt," she had explained, blushing even as she admitted this to the man she already trusted more than anyone in the world. "I don't know — I just don't like my asshole." She'd laughed self-consciously. "It's funny looking. I don't want anyone looking at it, or touching it."

Cam hadn't laughed at her, or teased her. He'd thought about what she said for a moment, and then replied, "I understand. A lot of people are shy about that, especially at first. First I will reassure you — your little asshole is perfect. It's beautiful, just like the rest of you." He had smiled and Marissa had found herself smiling back in spite of her misgivings. Cam had continued, "I view it as my duty as your Dom to help you move past any shyness or resistance where your body is concerned. The good news is that anal sex can be extremely pleasurable for both the giver and the receiver. And in your case, precisely because of your reservations, it will be a true test of your submission. A chance to allow your Master full access to every part of your body, not just the parts you're comfortable with." He'd kissed her gently, adding, "There will come a time, darling girl, when I will require you to submit in this way. And when I deem you're ready, you will give of yourself completely. Is that understood?"

When he talked like that, Marissa melted into a pool of submissive longing. She'd have been ready at that moment to spread her ass cheeks and beg him to fuck her, but she'd only nodded and whispered her agreement.

Tony let out a guffaw, which snapped Marissa back to the moment. "I don't think your slave girl likes anal," he said. "At least judging from the expression on her face right now."

"My slave girl," Cam replied with a confidence Marissa wished she shared, "does what she's told. She likes what pleases her Master, isn't that right, slave M?"

"Yes, Sir," Marissa answered honestly, though her stomach remained clenched with nervous anticipation.

"Good. Let's go up to the dais."

Marissa allowed Cam to lead her up the portable stairs to the platform. He stood in front of her, obscuring her view of Tony and Dana. Leaning close, he said in a low voice, "Remember, you are mine, and I will keep you safe. I'm going to have you run through a few positions, and then I'm going to use the smallest anal plug they make. Your only job is to follow my directives. Open yourself to me, both your spirit and your body. Trust me, and more importantly, trust yourself. You can do this. I know you can."

Marissa nodded. She closed her eyes and breathed in slowly, using the relaxation techniques Cam had taught over their time together. She replayed his words in her head: *Open yourself to me, both your spirit and your body. Trust me, and more importantly, trust yourself. You can do this. I know you can.*

Yes, she told herself firmly. *You can do this.* Aloud, she said, "Yes, Sir. I'm ready."

Cam stepped to the side and said in a louder voice, "We'll start with an inspection of your asshole. I want you to assume a forehead press, ass facing our guests. You will reach back and spread your ass cheeks. Hold that position until I tell you to move."

Oh god. Marissa suddenly had a hard time catching her breath. She felt a little faint.

Cam was regarding her with a solemn, patient expression. *I love you,* he mouthed silently.

His words were like sunlight, burning away the worst of her trepidation. He had said they would wait until she was ready. He must believe she was ready. She would believe it too, in a submissive leap of faith, both in Cam, and in herself.

Marissa sank as gracefully as she could to her knees. In a way it was better to be facing away from Tony and Dana. She could pretend she was alone with Cam. She lowered herself until her forehead was touching the floor. Reaching back, she gripped either side of her ass and spread her cheeks, glad no one could see her burning face.

She heard Cam descending the stairs. Time seemed to stand still as she held her position, her asshole bared for all to see. Finally Cam returned. She could hear him moving behind her. "Keep your position. This will feel a little cold."

He touched her anus with a gooey finger. Though she'd been expecting it, Marissa startled a bit at his touch. He was very gentle, moving just the tip of his lubricated finger in a circle before easing it gently into her ass. Marissa blew out a breath, willing herself to relax and receive her Master's touch. He wasn't hurting her. In fact, if she could get past her nerves and embarrassment, it felt kind of good.

"Now the plug," he said. "Stay relaxed for me. You're doing really well."

His finger was removed, and she felt the hard tip of the plug take its place. Again she tensed, and again she reminded herself to relax, to submit, to take what her Master was giving her.

She could feel the plug moving past the tight ring of muscle. It felt snug, but not painful. She could do this! Then, suddenly, a sharp pain shot through her rectum. She yelped and jerked forward.

"Stay in position," Cam said, his tone calm but firm. "That was the tough part. It's in now. You did it."

Marissa could feel the circle of soft rubber at the base of the plug between her ass cheeks, and she could imagine the lewd presentation she must be making. At the same time, a surge of warm pride moved through her. She'd done it!

Cam tapped her shoulder, the signal that she should rise. For a moment she was confused. She'd handled the butt plug. Now wasn't he going to remove it? She hesitated a moment, in case he'd forgotten, but he tapped again, adding, "Stand up, slave M. Turn around and face our friends in an at-attention position, hands locked behind your head."

Marissa forced herself to rise. The plug created a full but not unpleasant sensation inside her. She turned slowly and lifted her arms. Her heart was thudding but she felt excited, even exhilarated. Tony had his eye to the camcorder, which was trained on her. Dana had a big smile on her face. Again she held up her thumb in silent approval.

"You did exceptionally well, as I knew you would," Cam said, and Marissa couldn't stop the proud smile that spread over her face. "I know that was hard for you, slave M, but you overcame your own inhibitions and submitted with grace. I do believe a reward is in order. I'm thinking a flogging might fit the bill? Would that suit you?"

"Oh," Marissa replied happily. "Yes, Sir. That would suit me very well."

"Excellent. I have an idea, and you may decline if it's not to your liking. Tony and I were talking earlier, and we thought it might be a good experience if Tony were to flog you from behind while I stand in front of you. I've never actually gotten to watch your face when you fly, and I would love to see the transformation without the distraction of flogging you myself. What do you think?"

The thought of being able to look into Cam's beautiful eyes while she was being flogged by a skilled Master was deeply compelling, and Marissa readily agreed to the idea. Cam brought her to stand beneath hanging chains, to which he clipped the soft leather cuffs he'd given her as a gift their second time in his home dungeon. She lifted her arms, an erotic thrill coursing through her as Cam closed the cuffs around her wrists. He tightened the chains until her arms were fully extended overhead.

Tony and Dana were now seated to their left. Retrieving the flogger he'd selected earlier, Cam turned to Tony. "If you're ready?" he said, holding out the flogger.

Tony stood. "You bet." Bending over, he kissed Dana. "You take care of the recording, okay? I promise you'll get your turn afterward, my dear."

"I'll hold you to it," Dana said with a grin. "I'm feeling awfully squirmy watching these two. You know patience never was my strong suit."

Tony laughed. "You can say that again, sub girl," he said in a teasing tone. Marissa could feel the affection between them, and it made her smile.

Tony started with a nice warm up, slowly but steadily ratcheting the intensity, using more force on her ass. A few times the thongs landed so she felt the impact as it hit the rubber base of the butt plug, the vibrations moving up through her ass, as if she were being flogged from the inside out.

At first Cam just watched her, his muscular arms folded over his chest, his brilliant blue eyes moving over her body like fingers, leaving her warm and tingling with desire for him. She couldn't help but notice the bulge of his erection against the soft, black leather, and her mouth actually watered at the thought of worshipping his lovely cock once they got home.

A sudden, stinging stroke, much harder than those that had come before, made Marissa gasp with pain. The sting quickly eased into a pleasurable heat, but the stroke was followed by another, and then another, until pleasure and pain began to blur. Tony struck her shoulders, her back, her ass, her thighs, each stroke a thudding whack that made her sway in her chains.

Cam reached for her breasts, capturing her nipples and twisting. The sudden, sharp pinch distracted Marissa from the stinging onslaught behind her. "Ah!" she cried, wincing in her pain, though it shot paradoxically directly to her cunt, which throbbed with need.

Tony was focusing on her ass now, angling the flogger in such a way that the tips of each tress snapped like a thousand needles piercing her flesh. "No!" Marissa cried, though she hadn't meant to. "I can't. I can't!" Her feet began to dance in an involuntary effort to get away from the relentless onslaught against her burning flesh.

"You can," Cam said, his voice deep and commanding. "Do it for me, slave M. Suffer for your Master."

Those words! They were like a balm over her senses, and Marissa felt her body relax. Her feet stopped their involuntary dance and she stilled as she stared into Cam's eyes. He put a hand on her throat, his touch light but masterful. She shuddered, her eyes still locked on his. With his other hand, he reached between her legs. Gently he tugged at the small gold ring she wore there, the gesture reminding Marissa of the deep, abiding love she'd seen in Cam's eyes as the needle had slipped through her flesh. Releasing the ring, he slipped a finger into her sopping cunt. Marissa groaned, any lingering modesty gone now. She couldn't help herself as she leaned into his touch. He moved his hand, mashing his palm against her as she shamelessly ground against him, her clit hard as a pebble.

Tony finally stopped the stinging tip-flogging and shifted to the full, thuddy strokes Marissa loved. He was hitting her hard, as hard as she'd ever been flogged, but Cam's hand on her cunt and her throat, and his steady, loving gaze into her eyes made the flogging not only bearable, but perfect. It was what she needed. It was what she was born for.

"Yes, yes, yes, yes," she began to chant, only aware she was speaking when she heard the word bursting from her lips again and again. "Yes, yes, yes, yes…"

The pleasure became nearly unbearable, and the hard leather turned her skin to fire, while Cam's perfect touch reduced her to shuddering jelly. Her head fell back, her chant fading into steady, slow breathing. She sagged hard against her wrist cuffs, a low moan emerging from somewhere deep inside her. The first wave of a powerful orgasm crashed over her, leaving her momentarily stunned. Several more waves followed, one after the other rolling through her as the flogging continued, consuming her in its fire.

"That's it," Cam said from somewhere far away. "You're nearly there. Go. Now."

His word was her command, and Marissa let go of the last vestiges of her control. She tumbled into a deep, welcoming silence, as her spirit left her body and soared in a pure, perfect place that surely must be heaven...

When awareness returned to her, Marissa was cradled in Cam's arms on the floor. "You did good, baby," he crooned in her ear. "I'm so fucking proud of you."

Marissa leaned back in Cam's comforting embrace as she basked in his praise.

From somewhere to her left, she heard Dana say, "Hey, Tony, remember that movie *When Harry Met Sally?* I want what she's having!"

Chapter 10

Marissa filled her cup and added enough cream and sugar to mask the bitterness of coffee left too long on the warmer. The staff lounge was empty, and she moved toward the window to watch the traffic below as she sipped the tepid brew.

She heard the sound of someone entering the room behind her and for one delighted second she thought it might be Cam, coming in early before his evening shift to surprise her. But when she turned, it was the handsome, smug face of Phil Mitchell that greeted her. "Well, well," he said, opening his arms as if he expected her to come running into them. "Fancy meeting you here."

"Hello," Marissa said brusquely. She moved toward the sink and dumped what remained of the coffee, quickly washing her cup and placing it in the rack. She would have thought after the dreadful confrontation they'd had at the happy hour and her later undisguised annoyance at his intrusion into her office that the guy would want to steer clear of her, but it almost seemed as if he sought her out.

Until now she'd managed to avoid speaking to him since she'd come upon him snooping around in her office, but she'd seen him a number of times skulking around on the unit, when, as far as she knew, the software installation was complete on her floor. Several times she caught him staring at her in a way that made the tiny hairs on the back of her neck rise, but this was the first time she'd found herself alone in his presence.

Turning from the sink, Marissa started to move past Phil. He was standing between her and the door, hands in his pocket, a strange, unpleasant expression on his face. He shifted as she did, almost as if he were trying to block her from leaving. "Hey, Doc," he said, his smile edging into a leer, "where you off to in such a hurry? If I didn't know better, I'd say you were trying to avoid me."

Marissa frowned and looked at her watch. Could the guy really be that clueless? Or had he been so drunk at happy hour that he didn't remember how horribly he'd behaved? She had half a mind to tell him exactly what she thought of him, but she quickly thought better of it. With that kind of guy, it was better just to cut and run.

"Excuse me. I have an appointment." She pushed past him. She would be glad when the software installation and training were complete and she never had to set eyes on the asshole again.

That evening Marissa arrived home exhausted as always, but looking forward to Cam's arrival around midnight. Though they didn't get to spend much time together at the hospital, save for their professional interaction, Marissa hated the days when Cam had the evening shift, and didn't come on duty until her day was nearly over. Cam had been hinting it might be a good idea to move in together, and so far Marissa hadn't said yes or no, but she had to admit, she was definitely leaning toward a yes. The thought was at once exciting and a little scary. It would take things to a new level.

In their D/s relationship, each time Marissa had wanted something Cam offered, and at the same time been afraid, he had taken her by the hand and led her with such dominant confidence, respect and love to a new, better place. She knew in her bones she could trust Cam with her life. What more did she need to know?

She would tell him tonight. When he arrived, she would wrap herself around him and whisper in his ear that she was ready for the next step. Invigorated by the prospect, Marissa groomed herself carefully in the shower and put on the pretty new satin camisole and tap pant set she had recently bought, thinking with a grin how nice it would be when Cam removed it.

It was around nine when her doorbell rang, startling Marissa from the novel she was reading. Why was Cam so early? Did something happen at the hospital? And why wasn't he using his key?

The doorbell rang again, followed by a brisk knock. Marissa realized it probably wasn't Cam at all. It was probably Mrs. Baxter from down the hall wanting to borrow a cup of sugar or something.

Marissa slipped off the bed and reached for her robe, pulling it around her. She tied the sash as she headed into the living room. She put her eye to the peephole. Whoever was standing there was obscured by a huge bouquet of roses wrapped in green tissue paper.

Marissa smiled. Cam must have traded shifts, or gotten off early for some reason. How like her darling man to surprise her with flowers. He was such a romantic. Heart skipping with happiness, Marissa turned the deadbolt and reached for the doorknob. She pulled the door open and stepped back, her entire body alive with anticipation.

It wasn't Cam.

The man standing there was dressed in black T-shirt, black jeans and heavy black combat boots. Marissa's mind was clicking and stuttering in its effort to place the familiar but unwelcome face of the too-handsome blond. Meanwhile, her body was sending signals of its own. Her mouth had gone suddenly dry, and ice water had replaced the blood in her veins.

"Phil," she finally managed. She clutched her robe at the throat. "What are you doing here? How did you get in the building?"

"Aren't you going to invite me in?" he said, gesturing toward her with the flowers. "I got these just for you." His mouth twisted into an unpleasant smile.

Marissa's brain finally kicked into gear. There seemed to be no end to this asshole's unmitigated gall. "Look, Phil," she snapped, letting the anger show in her voice. "I don't know what you think you're doing. After the horrible way you behaved, I can't believe you have the nerve to just show up at my door like this. I didn't invite you here. I don't want your flowers. Please go away." Heart hammering, she was pleased at least her voice had come out firm and commanding.

As she spoke, she moved to close the door, but Phil shoved forward with his shoulder so hard that Marissa stumbled back as the door flew open. Phil came into the room. His eyes still on Marissa, he reached behind himself to shut the door, his fingers finding and turning the deadbolt.

His eyes were glittering, reminding Marissa of the crack addicts she'd treated during residency. "What's the matter?" Phil demanded. "Don't you like roses? Oh wait, I get it." He narrowed his eyes, his face twisting into a leer. "You prefer the thorns, am I right, you sick bitch?" He grabbed a rose from the bunch, dropping the rest of the bouquet to the floor. Marissa watched, horrified, as he ripped the flower from its stem and dropped the petals to the floor. He brandished the stem like a weapon as he advanced slowly toward her.

Marissa backed away, her heart beating so loudly she could barely hear Phil's bizarre words over the pounding in her ears. *The phone. Call 9-1-1.* Her phone was on the bedside table. She just had to get to the bedroom, lock the door, make the call.

She turned sharply from the intruder. She felt the tug on her robe and jerked away, allowing it to be pulled from her body as she made the dash toward the bedroom. She had nearly made it to the door when she felt him on her. His fingers dug into her shoulders as he spun her around. "Where do you think you're going, huh? You belong to *me* now. That faggot nurse isn't going to save you."

He mashed her face against his chest. Gripping a handful of her hair, he jerked her head back and pressed his lips against hers. He reeked of alcohol as he thrust his slobbery tongue into her mouth. Marissa tried to wriggle out of his hold, but he was too strong, one arm like steel around her waist, his fingers tugging so hard it felt like he might yank her hair out by the roots.

Finally he let her go, but only long enough to grab her shoulders and force her to turn around. Moving behind her, he propelled her into the bedroom. He kicked the bedroom door shut and threw her onto the bed.

Terrified but determined, Marissa scrabbled for her phone. Clutching it in a shaking hand, she pushed the button to activate the voice command. "Call nine-one—" she began, but before she could complete the words, Phil leaned over the bed and whacked her wrist with a karate chop that made her whole arm go numb. The phone fell from her grasp. Phil grabbed it and threw it across the room. It hit the wall with a thud and landed on the carpet.

"What are you doing," she gasped, tears of pain and fear nearly blinding her as she grasped her throbbing wrist.

"Exactly what you *want*, you twisted little cunt." He laughed cruelly as he loomed over her. "And to think, I actually bought that outraged prim and proper bullshit you spouted at that happy hour. *Oh Phil*," he said, his voice rising suddenly in a falsetto that was supposed to approximate a woman's voice, "*I'm not that kind of girl.*"

Marissa glanced toward the phone, now out of reach on the ground, desperately trying to think how to convince this nut job to get the fuck out of her apartment. He was obviously drunk, maybe high as well, on god knew what. Was he going to rape her? To kill her?

Don't let him see your fear.

Scrunched as far from him as she could get, still holding her wrist, Marissa strived to make her voice calm but firm. "Phil. Listen to me. I have no idea what you think you're doing, but it's obvious you've made a mistake. You seem to be confusing me with someone else. I didn't invite you here. You need to turn around now and go."

Phil shook his head and snorted. He pulled the messenger bag from his shoulder and tossed it onto the bed. "I didn't make a mistake. You did, babe.

Your first mistake was leading me on at the bar, batting your eyelashes and shoving your tits in my face like a regular little cock tease."

"I didn't—" Marissa began, but Phil sat abruptly on the mattress and leaned toward her, grabbing both her wrists, his face close to hers.

"Don't talk back," he snarled. "Slave girls don't talk back to their Masters."

Marissa realized her mouth had fallen open in her shock. Phil lifted an eyebrow and smiled an ugly smile. "That's right, I know all about your dirty little games, you filthy slut. I know all about the sick shit you and that pervy male nurse get up to, so you can cut the outraged innocence bullshit."

Marissa tried to swallow, but her tongue and throat muscles seemed to be paralyzed. Phil was gripping her wrists so tightly she was afraid he might actually break the bones. "Please," she finally managed to croak. "Let go of me. You're hurting me."

To her relief, he let her go, though he made no move to rise from the bed. Reaching for the messenger bag, he dumped out its contents. With a horrified glance, Marissa saw a ball gag, a set of metal handcuffs, several braided hanks of thin white rope, and a riding crop. What was this deluded monster planning?

Still hoping to somehow get away, Marissa slid toward the edge of the bed and tossed her legs quickly over the side. She would grab the phone and dash into the bathroom. She would lock the door and—

Drunk or not, Phil was faster than she was. His arm shot out and he easily pulled her back down onto the bed. As they struggled, Marissa frantically tried to knee him in the groin. "My boyfriend will be here any minute!" she shouted. "You better get the hell out right this second or—"

"Shut up, twat," he grunted, slamming her against the bed. "I have access to your hospital's entire data management system. You think I don't know your boyfriend's work schedule? I've got a couple of *hours* before he shows up. That is, *if* he shows up at all. Are you sure he isn't headed for that S&M game room you two like to hang out at?"

He reached almost lazily for the handcuffs with one hand, grabbing both her wrists in the other. How was this even happening? How did this maniac know the things he seemed to know? Marissa felt suddenly sick. Bitter bile rushed into her mouth and she had to swallow hard to keep from vomiting.

As she watched in horror, Phil placed one of the metal cuffs around her wrist and clicked it closed. She tried to jerk her other arm away, but she was no match for the strong man. He clicked the second cuff into place and grinned at her. "Panties wet yet, slut?"

Marissa was shaking like a leaf. "Why are you doing this? Please let me go." The enormity of what was happening finally hit her like a punch to the gut. Her voice rose to a squeak. "Please don't kill me!"

"Kill you?" Phil barked a laugh. "Why would I kill you? Don't you get it? I'm doing this for *you*. I'm playing to your kink, bitch. Don't pretend you don't love what's happening. This is what you fucking *live* for. Save the bleating little protests for someone who buys your lily-white holier than thou bullshit. We both know the real deal, Doc. We know what a cunt you truly are."

"Let me go! Let me go!" she shouted.

"Shut up!" Phil snapped. He reached for the ball gag and dangled it in front of her. "See this? If you make any more fucking noise, I'm going to shove this in your mouth, got it?" He smiled and shrugged, adding in a frighteningly reasonable tone of voice, "After all, we don't want to disturb the neighbors."

Marissa stared at the ball gag and pressed her lips closed. She had to reach this guy somehow, even if he was high as a kite. She knew who he was—how did he possibly think he was going to get away with this?

Unless... No! He'd said he wasn't going to kill her. She had to cling to that hope. Soon Cam would be here, and this nightmare would end...

Phil stood and reached for her arms, hauling her roughly to her feet. Holding her tightly, he glanced around the room, his eyes settling on the hook on the back of her closet door. He moved in that direction, dragging Marissa stumbling along with him. He reached for the nightgown hanging on the hook and tossed it to the ground. Grabbing Marissa's arms, he yanked her shackled wrists over her head as he pushed her back against the door. He forcibly guided her wrists back until the chain between the cuffs looped over the hook, effectively tethering her to the door.

"Don't move," he said sternly. "If you try to take down your wrists, I'll make you very, very sorry, you understand me?" As he spoke, he curled one hand around her throat. His grip was nothing like Cam's sensual touch, and instead of responding with a melting sigh of submission, Marissa gave a yelp of fear and squeezed her eyes closed, her mind a white, hot blank of terror.

I'm going to die. I'm going to die...

All at once the pressure eased and Marissa opened her eyes, weak with relief. Phil was staring down at her legs, disgust twisting his handsome features. "You filthy little pig," he sneered. "You pissed yourself!" His lips lifted into an ugly smile. "Oh my god," he said in a voice dripping with disdain, "don't tell me you're into golden showers too. Do your perversions have no end?"

Marissa glanced down at the wet satin of her new tap pants. She could feel the urine rolling down her legs, and tears of mortification and rage pricked against her eyelids. "You fucking bastard," she hissed, anger for a moment obscuring her terror.

"Can't you see you're scaring me to death? Let me down, now!"

Phil shook his head. "Who's going to make me, hmm?" His hand shot out and, flinching, Marissa instinctively jerked her head to the side. As a result, his open palm cuffed her hard on the ear, which rang from the force of the blow. She sagged against the hook that held her aloft. She kept her eyes closed, silently willing Cam to come and save her, though Phil was right—Cam wasn't due for at least two hours.

Phil crouched in front of her and yanked down her tap pants. Marissa didn't even try to stop him, not that she could have. He used the soiled pants to roughly wipe the urine from her legs and then tossed them aside.

"Nice," he said, drawing out the word. "I like a bald cunt. No nasty pubes to get in the way. Spread your legs so I can see what you got."

Marissa didn't move. He slapped her thigh hard. "I said spread your fucking legs, bitch." Miserably, Marissa obeyed. The position caused the handcuffs to tighten and she winced with pain as they pinched her skin.

"Holy shit, what is that?" Roughly he fingered the tiny, precious golden ring Cam had placed there. Marissa tried to slam her legs closed but he held them apart, digging his fingers into her thighs. "You really are one twisted bitch, you know that?" He tugged again at the ring.

"Stop it! You're hurting me! Don't touch me!" Marissa cried, tears of fury and embarrassment stinging her eyes.

Ignoring her, Phil slipped a hard finger between her labia and frowned. "What the hell?" he demanded. "Why aren't you wet? You live for this shit. I thought you'd be soaked by now."

How in god's name could this bastard think she'd get off on what he was doing?

And then it hit her.

Slave girls don't talk back to their Masters. I know all about you and your dirty little games, you filthy slut. I know all about the sick shit you and that pervy male nurse get up to...

"My laptop," she whispered, staring at him with dawning horror. "That day in my office. You did something..."

Phil looked up at her, his laugh derisive. "You're just figuring that out?" He shook his head. "Jesus, and here I thought MDs were supposed to be smart!" He stood, his face hovering close to hers. She squeezed her eyes to blot out the unwelcome sight as he breathed his whiskey breath in her face. "I know everything about you, slave girl. I know the disgusting porn sites you like to visit. I know the nasty stuff you get up to with Nurse Pervo."

He took a step back and reached with both hands for the neck of her camisole. He ripped the silky fabric down the length of her torso as if it were no more than tissue paper in his hands. His tongue flicked over his lips with reptilian rapidity as he ogled her bare breasts. He reached for them with both hands, grasping and twisting her nipples until she winced with pain. "Because I know what I know," he said in a soft, dangerous voice, "you're going to let me do just exactly what I want, whenever I want, and never say a fucking word, not now, not ever. You hear me?" He twisted harder. "Answer, slut!"

It was too much—her predicament, the pain, the threats, the terror. The last semblance of control burst like a bubble inside Marissa and erupted in a howl. "Ooooow!" Marissa wailed. "Stop it! Stop it! Let me down!"

"Damn it!" Phil shouted, fury mottling his face. "I told you to keep it the fuck down!" He sprinted back to the bed and returned a moment later holding the ball gag. He shoved it roughly against Marissa's mouth and then fumbled behind her head, catching her hair painfully in the buckle. He pulled it tight, forcing her mouth open with the foul-tasting rubber ball, which pressed her tongue back toward her throat.

Tears were running down Marissa's cheeks as she implored him with an unintelligible gurgle to let her go. Ignoring her garbled protests, Phil went back to the bed and returned with the riding crop. Shoving the handle in his back pocket, he reached for Marissa's arms, lifting them from the hook. He spun her around so she was facing the door and yanked her wrists up, again draping the taut chain over the hook. "You," he said, punctuating the word with a sharp smack of the crop against her ass, "are" — smack — "a very" — smack — "bad" — smack — "girl!"

The crop flew over her ass and thighs in a steady, hard rain of stinging leather — no erotic buildup, nothing even remotely sensual. At first Marissa tried to stay still, not wanting to let the bastard have the satisfaction of knowing he was hurting her. But after a while her feet began to dance of their own accord as she bleated ineffectually against the invasive gag. He hit her again, and again, and again without variation or finesse. It was a beating — pure and simple — and it went on and on, until Marissa felt as if she were being flayed alive.

Finally it stopped.

Marissa couldn't feel her hands or arms, and supposed she should be glad of that. She only wished her stinging ass were numb as well. Her chin and chest were wet with drool, her face streaked with tears. Her jaw ached from its forced and prolonged open position.

When Phil lifted her arms from the hook, they flopped heavily down, her lifeless cuffed hands hitting her in the stomach as she stumbled backward. He was just behind her, and he half-lifted, half-dragged her toward the bed. He threw her roughly down onto her stomach. Her arms and hands began to tingle painfully to life beneath her.

She felt the give of the mattress as he sat heavily beside her. When he flipped her over onto her back, she closed her eyes and turned her head away. She heard the click and then felt the relief of the metal cuffs being opened and lifted away. This was followed almost instantly by a sharp, throbbing bracelet of pain around each wrist. She stared down at the reddened, abraded skin, relieved at least to note there was no bleeding.

Phil tossed the cuffs carelessly aside and reached for a hank of rope. Marissa came suddenly alive, the possibility of escape once again leaping into her mind. If she could get off the bed and sprint to the bathroom, she had a pair of barber scissors in the drawer. She wouldn't hesitate to gouge the son of bitch's eyes out if she had to.

Girding herself, she rolled toward the edge of the bed, but hard fingers curling around her throat stopped her cold. "Where do you think you're going, young lady?" Phil snarled. "The party's just getting started." His fingers dug into the skin just below her jaw, effectively cutting off her ability to breathe and, like a cornered animal, Marissa froze in terror.

Keeping one hand tight around her throat, Phil unraveled a hank of rope single-handedly. He let go of her throat and Marissa gasped for air as he grabbed her throbbing wrists once more. He wound and knotted the rope around the damaged skin and then pulled her roughly upward on the bed. Jerking her arms over her head, he looped her wrists over one of the posts of her bedframe.

He reached for another hank of rope. Forcing her to spread her legs wide, he busied himself tying her ankles to the bottom posts. When he was done, he stepped back, his eyes raking insolently over her body. "You are hot, Doc. I'll give you that."

He reached for the hem of his T-shirt and lifted it over his head, shaking out his white-blond hair like a model on shoot as he flashed a movie-star perfect smile to the middle distance. He flexed his bulging biceps and pecs as if Marissa should admire his body. If she hadn't been gagged, she would have spit on him. Instead she just closed her eyes and turned her head away.

"Look at me, cunt!" Phil demanded. "I've got a better body than that faggot you hang out with. I can bench press two hundred and forty pounds. Not to mention, I'm built like a racehorse." She heard the sound his zipper sliding down. "I said, *look at me.*"

Not daring to refuse, Marissa turned her head again toward the monster holding her captive. She opened her eyes. Phil's jeans were down around his muscular thighs, a long, thick cock fisted in his big hand. He smiled a slow, arrogant smile. "And to think," he said with a grin, "this could have been yours, bitch." He stroked himself, his tongue again flickering over his plump lips, spittle gathered at the corners of his mouth.

"I'd fuck you," he continued, "but knowing what a dirty whore you are, I'm afraid my dick might fall off. Instead, you get to watch me come all over you. Keep your eyes open—you won't want to miss a single second, I'm sure."

Marissa stared at his face, shooting daggers with her eyes, her rage so palpable it made her entire body shake. Phil just smiled.

He moved closer, his hand now flying over his shaft. "Filthy cunt," he panted. "Dirty whore. Fucking sicko bitch." The words took on the tone of a chant interspersed with piggish grunts as Phil jerked off in front of her. When his eyes rolled back, Marissa shut her own eyes and tried to retreat to that quiet, safe place inside her where nothing and no one could hurt her, but the gag was too foul in her mouth, the drool soaking her chin, neck and chest, her wrists throbbing, her ass stinging, her outrage like a live thing skittering and slamming inside her.

Phil gave a loud groan and she felt the hot splash of his jism on her stomach, her breast, her cheek. "Aaaah!" he groaned. "That was good. So fucking good."

She opened her eyes to see him pulling up his pants. He reached for her face and Marissa tried to twist away, flinching in anticipation of whatever he was going to do next. He chuckled. "Relax, babe. I'm nearly done with you—for now."

He reached behind her and unbuckled the gag, pulling it from her mouth. Marissa opened and closed her aching jaw and tried, unsuccessfully, to wipe some of the drool from her chin onto the bed. Phil pulled his T-shirt back over his head and again shook his hair back with a practiced toss of his head.

He sat on the bed and untied her ankles. Marissa brought her legs together, watching mutely as he tossed the rope into the messenger bag. He picked up the handcuffs and the riding crop, placing them into the bag. Finally he released her wrists. Marissa grabbed at the sheet with shaking arms. She used an edge to wipe the man's disgusting ejaculate from her face and body. Then she curled in on herself on the far corner of the mattress, though she kept her eyes on her tormentor.

Phil put his hand into his jeans pocket. "That was fun, babe. Let's do it again sometime."

Marissa stared at the handsome monster standing in front of her. No matter what he knew, or thought he knew, about her, nothing would stop her from going to the police about this. Didn't he *know* that?

Apparently he did, because he said, his fingers moving in his pocket, "In here is my guarantee that you'll keep your pretty little mouth shut about what happened tonight. You've given me enough ammunition to assure not only your silence, but your ongoing cooperation." His mouth curved into an evil grin. "For a doctor, you're pretty fucking stupid, I have to say. Leaving all that stuff on your laptop." He shook his head with a look of amused disdain. "Don't you know what someone like me can do to someone like you?"

Marissa stared him, feeling sick. "It's simple," Phil continued blithely. "If you say a word about this to anyone, I'll destroy you. When I give your boss the information I've gleaned, you'll lose not only your cushy job, but that precious medical license of yours, mark my words. If you dare go to the cops, copies of your homemade porn video will be sent to the chief of staff at the hospital, as well as to the *New York Post* and the *New York Times*, plus I'll post it on YouTube. I have everything ready to go with the push of a button, babe. One false move on your part, and you can kiss your career and your reputation goodbye." He pulled something from his pocket and tossed it onto the bed. Hoisting the messenger bag over his shoulder, he added, "See you later, skank. Next time I better find you wet and ready."

Turning on his heel, he strode out of the bedroom. A moment later Marissa heard the click of the deadbolt, and then the door slammed.

She looked down at what he'd thrown onto the bed. It was a small red plastic rectangle with a sliver of metal showing on one end. It took her a moment to realize it was a computer flash drive.

Marissa's hand shot out, her fingers curling around the drive. Without realizing what she was doing, she hurled it with all her strength toward the wall. Then she fell back against her pillows, a dam bursting inside her as she curled in on herself and began to sob.

Chapter 11

Cam turned the key quietly in the lock in case Marissa was sleeping. When he'd left the hospital he'd been bone tired, but somehow each stop of the subway seemed to lift a layer of fatigue from his shoulders as it brought him that much closer to Marissa. By the time he'd reached her apartment building, he didn't even bother with the ancient, impossibly slow elevator, but instead took the stairs two at a time until he reached her floor.

When he stepped into the living room, he saw a bouquet of roses tightly wrapped in green tissue paper lying on the floor. A few feet away lay a single stem, its petals scattered nearby. While his brain struggled to process and provide a reason for such a strange sight, his body went into instant alert mode — his muscles tensing for a fight, his gut clenching into a fist.

"Marissa!"

He sprinted the short distance to her bedroom and pushed past the door, which was ajar. The room was lit only by the light emanating from the bathroom. Marissa was huddled in the center of the bed, curled in upon herself like a child. Something was very, very wrong.

Flying to the bed, he reached for her shoulders. "Marissa, what is it? What happened? Who was here? Did they hurt you?"

Marissa lifted a face swollen from crying, her eyes rimmed red, her lips trembling. Mutely she held out her wrists. Each was circled with red, ravaged skin, the marks of metal cuffs or very rough rope. Fear, fury, and the desperate need to know what had happened, however horrible the knowledge, clattered and jangled inside Cam in a cacophony of emotion.

"Oh my god," he whispered. "What happened to you? Baby, why didn't you call me? Did you call the police? Are you okay? Please, talk to me."

Marissa met Cam's eye. "I'm okay. I didn't call the police." She blew out a tremulous breath. "I don't want them involved. I wanted to call you but I didn't know what to say. He threatened if I told, he would...I didn't want... Oh Cam, I don't know what to do." She wrapped her arms around Cam's neck and began to sob.

He gathered her close against him and held her tight, tears spilling down his own cheeks as he gently rocked her in his arms. He forced himself to be patient, to let her cry, let her gather her thoughts, catch her breath. Finally she spoke in a whisper against his neck. "It was Phil. Phil Mitchell. He came here. He—it—what he did... It was horrible."

"Wait, what?" Cam was thoroughly confused. "That computer technician who has been putting in the new system at the hospital? *He* did this to you? I don't understand." Even as Cam tried to reconcile the image of the guy, who had been strutting around the unit for the past few weeks getting in people's way at their work stations and flirting with the female staff, with the person who had done this to his darling, he already knew he would hunt the bastard down if it was the last thing he did. It took every ounce of self-control not to roar out his pain and rage at the thought of someone entering Marissa's home and violating her, but Cam forced himself to remain outwardly calm for her sake. Now was not the time to go into macho bluster mode.

He extricated himself gently from her embrace. He took her face in his hands and looked deep into her eyes. "Tell me," he coaxed. "Tell me what happened."

Haltingly at first, and then faster and faster, the horrible words came tumbling over themselves as Marissa told Cam what that vile monster had done, and threatened to continue doing. As she spoke, the fear in her voice was edged out by anger, and her eyes sparked with the same fury that burned in Cam's gut.

"Jesus, Marissa," he swore when she was done. "We have to call the police! We can't let this guy get away with this."

"He got into my laptop, Cam. He knows about the training video. He has a copy."

"What? How the hell did he do that? What are you talking about?"

"I found him in my office a while back, and it was a day I had my personal laptop at work. He claimed he was just doing the software installation on the office PC, but I thought at the time something wasn't right." Marissa hugged herself miserably. "He left a flash drive here tonight to back up his threat. I haven't watched what's on it, but I'm pretty sure I know." Marissa pointed toward the wall. "I threw it over there somewhere. We should probably watch it to know for sure."

Cam rose from the bed and moved toward the wall, scanning the floor until he saw the red plastic flash drive in the corner. He picked it up between thumb and forefinger like it was a dead cockroach and returned to Marissa. "I'll watch it later, sweetheart. But whatever's on there, we still should let the police know, don't you think?"

"No. No police." Marissa crossed her arms across her chest. "We can't take the chance, Cam. This isn't just about me. You're involved too because of the video." She outlined Mitchell's threats if Marissa tried to take any action against him. "Phil has it all figured out. Even if I press charges and he's arrested, if this goes to trial, our names and reputations will be dragged through the mud in the process. At the very least we'll be publically humiliated, but we could end up losing our jobs over this, Cam. I don't think his threat was an idle one. It could destroy our careers."

Cam was quiet as he thought about what Marissa was saying. She was right about the potential humiliation, though he didn't care about himself. It was Marissa he was thinking of—of the relentless, invasive police questioning as they forced her to go over and over what had happened. And if it went to trial, it would become a matter of public record. Protected and somewhat insulated within the supportive BDSM community in which he was involved, Cam sometimes forgot just how judgmental and damning the outside world could still be regarding lifestyles they didn't understand.

He decided not to press the issue. He would respect Marissa's decision and support her in every way he knew how. Phil Mitchell could be dealt with later. Right now his focus must be on taking care of his girl.

Cam stood and lifted Marissa into his arms. He carried her to the bathroom and set her carefully on her feet. Closing the door, he turned on the shower. While the room began to fill with steam, Cam stripped off his clothing. He helped Marissa into the shower and stepped in beside her. Gently, soothingly, he washed her body from head to toe, soaping away every trace of that bastard, wishing he could expunge him from her mind as well. As he worked, he conducted a surreptitious exam to make sure she was really okay. He sucked in his breath when he saw the red marks on her ass, and the faint bruising showing just beneath the skin.

He shampooed her hair and held her as she stood beneath the hot spray, his heart nearly breaking with love and concern. Only when the water began to cool did he turn it off and reach for a towel. Wet and dripping himself, he dried Marissa, gently patting her skin while she stood, compliant as a child, her beautiful blue-green eyes fixed trustingly on his face. He draped another over her shoulders. Only then did he grab a towel for himself.

His arm around her, Cam led Marissa back into the bedroom. "Wait a second," he said, moving quickly toward the bed. The thought of that bastard touching the sheets, terrorizing Marissa, spurting his ejaculate over her and the bedding, made him want to vomit. Yanking back the rumpled linens, he stripped the bed to the mattress and tossed the pile into a corner. He placed his towel on the bare mattress and gestured for Marissa to lie down.

Opening her bedside night table, Cam took out the salve they used after intense play sessions. He applied it to her wrists, and then rolled her gently to her stomach so he could smooth the healing cream onto her ass and thighs. Marissa was resting with her cheek on her arms, watching his ministrations with a somber expression.

"You want to sleep, baby?" Cam asked. "I'll remake the bed with fresh sheets. Can I get you something to drink? Water, brandy?"

Marissa rolled over and sat up. She shook her head adamantly. "No. I don't want to stay here. I know it's late, but can we go to your place?"

Cam nodded. "Absolutely. I'll call a cab right now." They dressed quickly. While Marissa was in the bathroom brushing out her hair, Cam slipped the flash drive into his jeans pocket.

On the ride to his house, Cam said, "You know, that asshole is not going to get away with this. I understand you don't want to involve the cops, but maybe there's another way..." He trailed off as he said this, the seed of an idea forming in his mind. He thought about the old adage—*don't get mad, get even.* Turning to Marissa, he said, "So Mitchell threatened to send a copy of our private training video to Dr. Hession?"

Marissa, who had been looking out the cab's window, turned back to face Cam with a frown. "I don't know him all that well, but from what I can tell, Fred Hession is a very straitlaced guy. Very conservative. He'd probably fire us on the spot."

Cam raised his eyebrows, a ghost of a smile lifting his lips.

"What? What's funny about that?" Marissa demanded, a touch of her natural spark returning.

"Just thinking of your characterization of Fred as a straitlaced guy. He does favor straitjackets, and would probably like a bit of lace as well. I know he loves silk and very high heels."

Marissa wrinkled her nose in confusion. "What are you talking about? You know Dr. Hession personally?"

"I do." Cam nodded. "In fact, I trained him."

Marissa continued to stare at Cam uncomprehendingly. "Trained him?"

Cam nodded. "Normally I wouldn't say anything, but these are extenuating circumstances so I think you should know. Fred is a member of The Power Exchange. He and his wife Lillian are regulars. She's a homemaker and his fulltime Mistress." Marissa's mouth had fallen open, her eyebrows rising higher and higher as he spoke. "In fact, that's how I got an interview at the hospital. Fred recommended me."

"Wow," Marissa finally said. "I had no idea."

"Why would you? It's his personal business. Same as us." Cam reached for Marissa's hand and gave it a comforting squeeze. "We don't have to deal with this alone, baby. And we're definitely not going to take this lying down. I understand and respect your wish not to involve the authorities. We'll handle this on our own, with the strength of the BDSM community behind us. When we're done with him, Phil Mitchell will wish he'd never been born."

Once home, Cam poured them each a large snifter of brandy, which they carried to the bedroom. Snuggled between the sheets, Cam took Marissa's hand. "Sweetheart, we need to tackle this right away, before that bastard does any more harm. I have the beginnings of a plan, and I want to call Jack Morris to get his input. Is that okay with you?"

Two spots of scarlet appeared on Marissa's cheekbones, but she nodded. "Yeah. It's okay. He should know that a video of the inner room is floating around out there. But it's after two. The club is closed tonight. Won't he be asleep?"

"Jack?" Cam shook his head. "He's an inveterate night owl. He jokes that he has vampire blood—only goes down when the sun comes up." Sure enough, Jack answered his phone on the second ring, recognizing Cam's number and answering in his booming bass, "Hey there, trainer. You pull the late shift at the hospital or something?"

With a glance and sad smile at Marissa, Cam explained briefly what had transpired. He held the phone away from his ear as Jack began to shout.

What's he saying? Marissa mouthed. Cam switched the audio to speaker and set the phone on the bed between them.

"—won't get away with this, that little piece of shit! Say the word, Cam, and that cocksucker will disappear. I still know guys who know guys, if you understand me."

"No," Marissa interjected. "Jack, it's Marissa. Listen, we don't want anything like that. I just want to make sure we stop him from doing any more damage. And we have to make sure he never does this to anyone else."

Jack reluctantly agreed, becoming enthusiastic again when Cam discussed the rudiments of the idea that had been germinating in his brain since the cab ride. They talked back and forth for quite a while, firming up the plan.

~*~

Phil Mitchell looked at himself in the mirror and grinned at his reflection. He was still stoked from the events of last night. He'd waited up late after he left her, just in case the bitch was stupid enough to call the cops, but the night had passed uneventfully, as had the morning. Neither Marissa nor her faggot boyfriend had showed up at the hospital so far, which was well and good. Even if Cam Wilder knew what had happened, what could he do? They were probably cowering together in their S&M lair with no idea what to do. Phil had them both over a barrel, and they knew it. He owned Marissa Roberts' ass now, and the fun was just beginning.

Everything had come together perfectly last night—from the seriously excellent cocaine he'd snorted that had made him feel like a god, to Wilder's working the night shift, to the helpful old lady who had let him into Marissa's apartment building when he pretended to fumble for his key. The expression on Marissa's face had been priceless when he'd tossed that flash drive onto her bed. It served her right.

People who played those sick, twisted sex games and then had the stupidity to record them deserved exactly what they got.

He had timed it perfectly, too, since today was his wrap up at St. Beatrice Hospital. All the software systems were enabled and working beautifully. He had an appointment with the chief of staff to give him the final report, and then it was on to another project.

Phil turned slightly to change the mirror angle and admired himself from the side. He really had an excellent jawline. The suit jacket hid his muscular build, but the padded shoulders compensated. He faced the mirror once more and buttoned the jacket, glad he'd sprung for the extra tailoring to highlight his trim physique.

The bathroom door opened and a janitor shuffled in pulling a wash bucket on wheels, a mop slung over his shoulder. Phil nodded a greeting and slid past him. He mustn't keep Dr. Hession waiting.

Phil strode purposefully down the corridor, smiling at the pretty nurses he passed. He winked at the fat broad—Janet, Janice—he couldn't quite remember—as he approached, and she giggled and simpered. *In your dreams*, he thought as he walked by.

"Hi. I have an eleven o'clock appointment with Dr. Hession," Phil told the plump, middle-aged secretary who was pretending to be busy at her desk.

She looked up at him with a sour expression. He flashed her a heart-stopping smile and she melted, just like they all did. "Oh yes," she gushed. "You can go right in. He's expecting you."

Phil knocked lightly on the ajar door and peered inside. Dr. Hession looked up. "Please, come in."

Phil entered the office and approached the older man's desk. He opened his leather portfolio and extracted the final report for the hospital. "Here's a summary of the work that's been done," he said, placing the pale gray folder with the words *HIF Software Solutions* typed on the cover in front of Dr. Hession. "Everything went very well. All software updates are in place, and the new system is fully operational. Your staff has been trained, but of course we'll be available to help with any questions, or to fix any bugs that might arise."

Dr. Hession glanced at the papers Phil had placed in front of him. Phil doubted he even knew what he was looking at—medical professionals could be so one-dimensional, focused only on their tiny, specific area of medical expertise, with blinders on for anything else. This actually suited Phil, since fewer questions and demands meant he could get on to the next job that much more quickly. If he occasionally cut a few corners in the process, no one was the wiser.

Dr. Hession looked up. "We're pleased with the job HIF has done for this hospital. I actually wanted to see you on another matter."

Phil felt a sudden jab of unease. Could that skanky bitch have been dumb enough to come to her boss in a preemptive move? Even as the thought crossed his mind, Phil dismissed it. She wouldn't be that stupid. Still, he blew out a breath he hadn't realized he'd been holding when Dr. Hession said, "You've done such a good job, I was wondering if you'd be interested in doing some work for an associate of mine. It's a small computer job—really something you could do on your own time, I would imagine. No need to involve HIF unless you thought it necessary. I have an entrepreneur friend who needs a management information system set up for one of his startups." He smiled at Phil. "Would you be interested in something like that?"

Phil could see the dollar signs parading in his head, and had to restrain himself to keep from rubbing his hands together. In point of fact, his contract with HIF precluded this sort of side job, but what they didn't know... "You bet," he said a little too eagerly. Tamping it down, he added in a sober tone, "Of course, I'd need to know more about it, but I'm sure I can work something out. Do you have his card?"

"I have a better idea." Dr. Hession stood and moved around his desk. "Do you have some time? How would you like to meet him right now? I can take you over to my club and introduce you. We could have lunch."

Phil grinned. A fancy lunch at a country club on someone else's dime, and the chance to make some serious cash on the side. The day was getting better and better. "Sounds like a plan," he said.

~*~

Both Marissa and Cam were taking a personal day, with Fred Hession's blessing. Marissa was spending the day with Dana, who insisted on canceling all her appointments as soon as she'd heard what had happened. Before heading out that morning, Cam had waited for Dana, who arrived within the half hour armed with hot coffee and muffins. Cam had felt better leaving Marissa with her good friend.

Tony and Jack sat with Cam at a table in the large, empty outer room of The Power Exchange. It felt strange to sit in the empty club in the middle of the day. Jack was dressed in a black muscle T-shirt, black cargo pants and black square-toed boots. With his shaved head and the grim expression on his grizzled face, he looked every bit the enforcer. Jack's cell phone buzzed. He looked down at it the screen. "They're on their way."

"Excellent." Tony, impeccably dressed in a tailored suit and silk tie, picked up the document he had just read to the others and folded it lengthwise. He slipped it into an inner pocket of his jacket.

Ten minutes later the front door buzzed and Jack strode to press the intercom button. "It's Fred Hession and guest," came a disembodied voice through the speaker. Jack released the lock to the door at the top of the stairs. He opened the door to the club and returned to the table. "I still think we ought to dispense with the charade and just beat the little shit into a pulp."

Tony shook his head. "It's always better if you get them to sign on the dotted line before anything else. If we get him to admit culpability on paper, our case will be that much tighter in the event of any future legal action."

"Spoken like a lawyer," Jack growled.

Tony shrugged. "Guilty as charged."

Cam pushed back from the table and stood. Rage simmered inside him like a corrosive acid. Though his head agreed with Tony, his gut agreed with Jack. His muscles were coiled, his hands aching with the need to feel the crunch of bone as he brought his right fist into the guy's jaw and followed it with a sharp hook designed to break the cocksucker's nose. Still, he knew it was better to stick to their plan. "See you in a few," he said. As he heard the sound of the men's feet clomping down the concrete stairs to the club, he walked quickly toward the back of the room and stepped behind a partition so he was hidden from view.

A moment later he heard Fred Hession's voice. "Come on over and I'll introduce you," he was saying. Cam could just imagine Phil Mitchell's confusion as he took in the space — the sumptuous country club-like surroundings, interspersed with the BDSM punishment circles that contained whipping posts, chains, stocks and St. Andrew crosses.

"What kind of a place is this?" Mitchell said, his voice cracking a little.

"Come sit down and we'll tell you all about it," Fred said. Cam shifted slightly so he could see around the partition. Jack and Tony got to their feet as Fred and Mitchell approached the table. Fred, Mitchell and Tony sat down. Jack remained standing. Cam stepped quietly out from behind the partition.

An edge came into Fred's voice, though a thin veneer of cordiality still remained. "Jack, Tony, I'd like you to meet Phil Mitchell, the scumbag who broke into Marissa's home, terrorized and violated her, and then threatened to blackmail her to keep her quiet."

Cam strode quickly to join the group. Mitchell turned in his chair at the sound his approach. His expression was one of almost comic confusion, his mouth hanging open, his eyebrows shooting up his forehead. His eyes bugged as he took in the sight of Cam, who it was clear he recognized. "What the fuck..." Mitchell pushed back his chair and jumped to his feet.

As if they'd choreographed it, Cam and Jack stepped on either side of the man, each clamping a heavy hand on his shoulder. Together they forced him back into the chair. The leather portfolio he'd been holding fell to the ground. Fred leaned over and picked it up.

"What the damn hell do you think you're doing? What is this? What's going on here?" Mitchell tried to rise, but Cam and Jack held him down. "Give me that." Mitchell gestured toward the iPad. "That's mine."

Fred folded his hands over the tablet. "I think not," he said calmly.

"What's going on here?" Mitchell demanded. "These aren't prospective clients. You got me here under false pretenses. This is some kind of setup."

"The boy's about as sharp as a bag of wet hair," Jack said dryly.

Mitchell twisted back to glare at Cam. "What're *you* doing here? What is this place? Let go of me! Goddamn, I said let go!" Cam could hear the fear beneath the bluster.

"I advise you to listen to what we have to say," Tony interjected in an authoritative voice. "That is, if you don't want to spend the rest of your life in prison."

His words seemed to have an effect, because Mitchell stopped jerking in their grip as he turned back to the table. "What's all this about? I have no idea what you're talking about," he lied.

"Allow me to enlighten you," Tony said. "I'm going to read a document that outlines your position.

You're going to listen, and then you're going to sign on the dotted line."

"I'll listen," Mitchell said in a tight voice, "because I have no choice." He stiffened again in their grip. "But I'm not signing shit."

"We'll see about that," Tony said with a cold smile. He reached into his jacket and pulled out the document he'd prepared earlier. He began to read. "'I, Phillip Mitchell, did knowingly and in violation of the law and of the terms of agreement between HIF Software Solutions, my employer, and St. Beatrice Hospital, our client, place an illegal capture device on the personal laptop of Dr. Marissa Roberts while said laptop was in her office at the hospital.'"

"Hey, you can't prove—"

"Shut up or I'll shut you up," Jack growled.

Cam squeezed his shoulder. "Christ, you're hurting me," Mitchell gasped. Cam didn't let up.

Tony continued as if there had been no interruption. "'I forced my way into Marissa Roberts' personal residence, wherein I proceeded to molest, terrorize, torture and threaten her for nearly two hours. I attempted to coerce Dr. Roberts into silence about what I'd done, threatening that if she told anyone, I would publish a private, personal video I had stolen from her laptop, as well as reveal the nature of said video to the hospital's chief of staff, Dr. Frederick Hession, with the express intent of causing her to lose her job and her license to practice medicine.'"

"Lies! All a pack of lies!" Mitchell twisted back once more toward Cam, his eyes rolling with fear and rage. "She came on to *me*. I know it's hard to hear it, but your little girlfriend is a cock tease. She invited me to her place. It was all consensual. Whatever she said, it's her word against mine. And anyway, I have the video of you two perverts that will—"

"Shut up," Cam said in a voice dark with fury. "Shut. The. Fuck. Up." He realized he wanted to kill Phil Mitchell, and the awareness caused him let go of Phil's shoulder as if the man were on fire. He took a step back. Mitchell must have seen something in Cam's face, because he paled and finally shut his mouth. Jack met Cam's eye and something in his calm expression penetrated the rage. Cam swallowed and nodded, feeling somewhat back in control.

"I'm okay," he said in answer to Jack's unspoken question. Jack nodded.

Tony continued. "'I know there is no way to undo the heinous crimes I have committed, but I am willing to make full restitution. First, I agree to be punished for my actions and humbly ask that Master Jack Morris mete out said punishment, which I am aware I richly deserve. Furthermore, I fully approve of the recording of said punishment, the full rights of the recording which I assign without limit or reservation to Master Jack to do with as he will.'"

"What? What the hell? What are you saying?" Phil croaked, his voice cracking.

"I'm not done yet," Tony said. "But hang on. We're nearly there." He continued reading. "'I further grant Master Jack full access to my place of work and to my home. I will allow him to thoroughly search the premises, and to remove any item he deems offensive or to have been acquired illegally.

"'Finally, I agree to resign my position at HIF Software Solutions, effective immediately. Once I have permission from Master Jack to leave, I agree that I will move out of the state of New York, and I will never return.

"'If it is determined at any time, now or in the future, that I have broken any of the stipulations contained herein, I understand that civil and criminal charges will be brought against me for my wrongdoing, and that I will be prosecuted to the fullest extent of the law.'" Tony held out the pen.

"You're out of your fucking minds! This is duress! That contract would never stand up in a court of law!"

"Are you refusing to sign?" Tony said.

"You bet your ass I'm refusing—"

Jack looked at Cam, talking over Mitchell's outraged splutter. "You heard the man. I guess we have no choice."

"Agreed."

Together they hauled the bastard to his feet. Tony and Fred also stood and moved toward them. Though Mitchell struggled, the two of them together were stronger than he was, and they got him past the bar and into the inner room, Tony and Fred following closely behind.

They dragged the shouting man toward the St. Andrew's cross they'd agreed upon earlier and forced him into position facing the cross. Cam and Jack each grabbed an arm. They wrenched them up and held them against the cross as Tony wrapped a thick Velcro cuff around each wrist.

Jack moved behind Mitchell and squatted. He pulled off Mitchell's loafers, barely seeming to notice when Mitchell's foot made contact as he kicked and squirmed. Standing, Jack reached around Mitchell's waist. He unbuckled the man's belt and unzipped his fly. Hooking his thumbs in the waist of Mitchell's pants, he yanked them down the man's legs and pulled them away, tossing them into a heap on the ground. Mitchell was screaming bloody murder the whole time.

Ignoring his protests, Jack kicked Mitchell's legs roughly apart. Tony and Cam knelt on either side of the cursing, snarling man and forced his ankles into the cuff restraints at the bottom of the X.

Mitchell's voice had risen high in his panic and his rage. "Goddamn it," he squealed, "you fucking perverts, let me down this second! You have no right to do this! Let me down!" He let loose a stream of invective as he struggled fruitlessly in his bonds.

"I've had enough of his mouth," Jack growled. "Gag him."

Cam moved toward the gear cabinet and retrieved the biggest ball gag in the drawer. Returning to Mitchell, he jerked his head back by the hair and pushed the gag roughly into his mouth. He buckled it tightly around the man's head.

Mitchell's shouts and curses were muffled to a pitiful gurgling. His face was beet red, his eyes rolling wildly in his head.

Cam felt a moment's conflict. The inner room was almost a sacred place in his mind, and a basic tenant of his BDSM philosophy included consent and respecting limits. How did what they were doing fit in with that?

Then the image of Marissa as he'd found her last night, her body torn and bruised, the terror in her tearful eyes, loomed large in his mind. This vicious, lying sack of shit had done damage it might take years to undo. He'd created wounds that might heal and scar over in time, but could never be forgotten. What they were doing now wasn't about consensual and loving BDSM. They were just using the location as a means to an end. It was the best way to reach this monster and hurt him where he lived.

Cam leaned close and murmured in Mitchell's ear. "Do you think you're as scared now as Marissa was last night? Did it make you feel like a man to overpower and terrorize a woman, you pathetic piece of shit? How does it feel to be bound and gagged against your will? Welcome to the inner room, asshole."

Fred, who was standing in front of the cross, reached into his jacket and removed his smart phone. He pushed a button and held it up. "Smile," he said to Mitchell. "You're on Candid Camera." He kept the phone aloft.

"The bastard used a crop on Marissa, is that right, Cam?" Jack said as he moved toward the whip rack.

Cam nodded. Jack returned with a long-handled crop. He held it toward Cam. "Care to do the honors?"

Cam stared at the crop. "No," he said quietly, recalling the bruises on Marissa's ass. "I'm afraid I couldn't stop."

Jack nodded his understanding. While Fred continued to record, Jack stepped to the side of the bound man and brought the crop down hard, leaving a neat red rectangle on his white ass. Mitchell jerked and yelped against the rubber ball in his mouth. Jack hit him again, leaving an identical mark on the other cheek.

Jack cropped the bastard until his ass was bright red, his body slick with fear sweat. Finally satisfied, Jack dropped the crop on the counter for later sterilization and returned to the cross. The four men lined up in front of Mitchell, who sagged in his cuffs, drool dripping down his chin, hate in his eyes.

Mitchell started to struggle again, his shouts emerging incomprehensibly behind the ball gag.

"Feels pretty shitty, doesn't it?" Cam said, letting his cold hatred seep into his words. "Being used like this against your will by someone you despise, and then threatened into silence. Payback's a bitch, ain't it?"

"Maybe he's learned his lesson," Jack said. He reached for the buckle of the ball gag and pulled it open.

Mitchell pushed the gag out with his tongue, drool streaming down his chin. "Let me down! Goddamn it to hell, let me the fuck down, you freaks!"

"I don't think his punishment was sufficient," Tony commented drily.

"I have to agree," Jack said. "He does seem a little slow. I guess we'll just have to put the gag back and try again—"

"No!" Mitchell cried, jerking his head from side to side. He took a deep, shuddering breath. "Please, no. Don't do that. Please. I'm begging you." His voice cracked and tears sprang to his eyes, which he blinked back angrily. "Let me down. Just let me down."

Tony took a pen out of his jacket and held it, along with the document, in front of Mitchell. "You ready to sign then?"

"You're out of your fucking mind if you think I'll sign that thing," Mitchell snarled.

"Maybe a little cock and ball torture will change his mind," Fred suggested. "We could tie him down to the exam table. We should probably shave his pubes first." He moved closer to Mitchell. "Tell me, do you like needles?"

Mitchell's face paled, sweat beading on his upper lip and forehead. "Christ," he murmured. "This can't be happening."

"Oh, it's happening, all right," Jack assured him. "And we have all day, boy. We're committed to the task of teaching you a lesson. How long it takes you to learn it"—he shrugged—"that's up to you."

"We could always use the strap-on. I bet Phil loves a good ass reaming, am I right?" Tony said with a grin.

"Excellent idea." Jack moved toward the gear cabinet. "I don't think we'll bother with the lube though. Real men don't need lube."

"Wait!" Mitchell screamed in alarm. "Okay, okay, okay! I'll sign the fucking thing."

The four men returned to stand in front of Mitchell. "You agree to all the stipulations?" Tony said.

"Yes. Yes, I said I'd sign it."

"You'll give Jack the keys to your office and your home? You'll quit your job and move out of this state?"

"Yes. I said yes, damn it. I want to get as far away as I can from the likes of you."

"We'll be watching you," Jack said. "Before I bought this club, I used to be in enforcement. I know people, if you follow me." He let the implied threat of his words linger in the silence a moment, and then added, "One false move, we'll be on you like white on rice."

"I got it, I got it!" Mitchell cried. "Just let me down. Let me out of here."

Jack nodded toward Cam, who moved to the cross and unstrapped Mitchell's right wrist. Tony moved closer, again holding out the pen and the piece of paper. Fred helpfully placed Mitchell's confiscated iPad underneath it.

With a shaking hand, Mitchell scrawled his signature at the bottom of the page.

Chapter 12

A low, plaintive moan wove its way through Cam's dream, jerking him from sleep. He bolted upright and reached for Marissa, who was thrashing beside him, the sheets twisted around her.

"Marissa. Marissa, wake up. Hey, wake up. It's only a dream."

Marissa's eyes remained screwed shut as she twisted out of his grasp. "Don't touch me!" she cried.

"Marissa. Stop it. It's me. You're safe. You're here with me, sweetheart. Wake up. Please, wake up." Cam pulled Marissa into his arms. He could feel her heart pounding, and her skin was damp with sweat.

Finally she opened her eyes and looked up into his face. "Oh, Cam," she whispered, her face crumpling.

"It's okay, baby," he crooned, cradling her against his chest. "It's okay. It's all okay now."

But was it?

It had been nearly a week since they had booted Phil Mitchell out of town. Marissa had claimed to be fine, citing her credentials as a medical professional that enabled her to process the situation, her three visits to the hospital psychologist who dealt with grief and trauma, and her awareness that Mitchell was no longer a threat in their lives. She hadn't slept at her apartment since that bastard had forced his way in, which Cam completely understood.

Cam was more than ready for her to officially move in, but decided to give her a little more time before broaching the subject. He didn't want to undermine her recovery by making her somehow think he was suggesting she should be afraid of living alone.

He decided instead to focus on resuming their D/s exploration, which up until the trauma, had been such a source of intensity and pleasure for them both. But now Marissa, who before had been so wonderfully eager to push the erotic envelope, seemed to have closed up like a flower in the dark, tightly furled and shut off from the joy of submission.

Instead she threw herself into her work with a vengeance, leaving the house at dawn to go to her club, then spending ten to twelve hours every day at the hospital, and working on her computer when she came home at night to catch up on her charts. She had fallen into bed each night this week claiming exhaustion, and Cam knew she wasn't lying about that. But he also knew she was using it as an excuse to keep him at arms' length, both physically and emotionally.

He wanted to be patient, and he understood she needed time to heal, but he also knew the longer she held herself apart, the harder it would be for them to reconnect. Something had to change, and he understood he would need to be the one to effect that change.

Now he just held her and stroked her damp hair away from her face. "Go back to sleep, sweetheart. I'll hold you and keep you safe." She smiled, and lifted her face to his, closing her eyes for a kiss. He kept vigil for a long time, until he was certain she was asleep. Only then did he close his own eyes.

"Tomorrow," he promised himself, "I'll talk to Jack. He'll know what to do."

~*~

Marissa pumped furiously on the elliptical, arms and legs working in concert as she approached the thirty-minute mark. Dana, who had finished her workout a minute before, stood beside her machine toweling the sweat from her face. "Have time for a quick fruit juice after your shower?"

Marissa looked down at her friend, glanced at the wall clock and shrugged. "I guess so."

They met up twenty-five minutes later at the exercise club's small café. As they sipped fresh orange juice, Dana said, "So, how's it going? I've barely seen you this week. You doing okay?"

Marissa glanced away as she answered. "Fine. I'm doing fine. Work is a good distraction. And Cam's been great."

Dana nodded. "So we'll see you at the club tonight?"

Marissa shook her head. She could feel the traces of a headache coming on. "Cam's got a client. I'm just going to stay home and get a good night's sleep."

"Marissa."

"What?"

"I've known you a long time. You're not okay."

Unwelcome tears pricked at Marissa's eyelids and she blinked them away, annoyed. "Nonsense. I'm fine. I've been seeing a counselor. Everything's good."

"Marissa."

"What?" Marissa let the impatience slip into her voice. "I told you. I'm fine." She finally looked directly at Dana, and was annoyed to see she was smiling.

"What? What's so amusing?"

"Your insistence that you're fine, when I know you're not."

Again Marissa started to protest, but Dana stopped her with a held up hand. "Marissa. Shut up for a second and listen. I want to ask you a question, and I want your honest answer."

Marissa tensed but nodded. "Okay."

"When is the last time you scened with Cam? When is the last time you were properly whipped?"

"Dana!" Marissa hissed, glancing at the tables around them, though no one appeared to be paying them any attention.

"Answer the question."

"Well. Not since…before. I've been too busy," she rushed on defensively.

"There is nothing more important right now." Dana reached for Marissa's hand.

"Give me a break. I mean, I haven't exactly been in the mood to play, you know," Marissa replied, but she didn't pull her hand away.

"I'm not talking about play." Dana's voice was gentle but earnest. "I'm talking about sustenance. About the life-giving submissive experience your Master can give you, if you let him. You know in your bones exactly what I'm talking about. For people like you and me, there is nothing more centering, or more essential, than being brought back to our core essence. It's what you were missing all your life until you found the courage to explore this key aspect of what and who you are, Marissa. And now that you've found it, you need to hold on to it. You need to nurture it and let it continue to grow. Don't shut Cam out of your life. Not now. Especially not now."

Marissa started to protest, to explain that she was essentially living with Cam now, and they'd never been closer. She wanted to refute Dana's claim that she was shutting Cam out of anything, but the words wouldn't come.

Because she knew, when she quieted the rest of the noise in her head, that Dana was right.

~*~

"How's she doing? How're you doing?" Jack was wiping down the bar in the still-empty club in the hour before it opened. Cam sat on the stool opposite him, waiting for his new client.

"Fine," Cam answered automatically. He looked up to see Jack regarding him with those dark, penetrating eyes. "Not so fine," he amended with a sigh. He told Jack about Marissa's avoidance of intimacy, and his own uncertainty in the face of it. "I love her so much, Jack. I don't want to cause her any more pain. I don't want to push her before she's ready."

"Let me ask you something." Jack put the washrag aside and focused his full attention on Cam. "If you were her trainer, not her lover, or no—let's not even talk about Marissa and you. If a client came in to see you, and told you she was new to the scene, but had found her soul mate, and D/s had become a central focus of her life, but a recent traumatic event had made her unsure about continuing, what would you say to that client?"

Cam didn't even have to think about the reply. "I'd say BDSM would be the very best cure for whatever ails her. I'd explain to her that what happened has less than zero to do with BDSM, with the intensity, the exchange of power, the passion."

"And you'd be right," Jack replied. "And then you'd probably contact her Master, am I right? And you'd tell him…"

Cam chuckled admiringly. Jack made what had seemed so muddled in his head suddenly crystal clear. "I would tell him it was his responsibility to his sub to quit handling her with kid gloves, and to give her what she needed — what they both needed."

Jack pointed a finger at Cam. "Bingo."

~*~

The next morning after a leisurely breakfast at an outside café, Cam announced, "We're going to run a little errand in Manhattan. There are few things we need to pick up for later."

"Where're we going?" Marissa asked with what seemed to be genuine eagerness.

"It's a place called C&C's in the Village. You'll love it."

When they came out of the subway on St. Marks, Cam led Marissa along the street and down the few stairs to the basement-level BDSM gear shop, tensing slightly in case she balked. His talk with Jack the night before had galvanized him, and he was determined to show Marissa she had nothing to fear, and everything to gain, from resuming their D/s love affair.

He was relieved when she offered no protest, as he was eager to introduce her to Celia and Cat. The familiar jingle greeted him as he pushed the door open and ushered Marissa inside.

"Oooh," Marissa breathed, as she took in the small but crowded space, filled with BDSM gear, jewelry and clothing. Celia was at her usual post behind the glass counter. Cat, a tall, statuesque woman with very short blond hair and large brown eyes, turned as they entered the store, her face breaking into a bright smile.

"Master Cam!" she enthused, moving forward to wrap him in a hug. "Celia said you'd been by a while back. It's about time you showed your face again."

Cam laughed. "I know. It's been too long. I'd like you to meet my partner and sub girl, Marissa," he said, pride blooming inside him as Marissa slipped her hand into his. He turned to her. "This is Mistress Cat, and that's Celia, her partner—"

"And sub girl," Cat interrupted. "Though you wouldn't know it from her sass." In spite of her words, she looked fondly at Celia, who this week sported bright orange hair with purple tips. Cat turned back to Marissa with a welcoming smile. "It's a pleasure to meet you, Marissa." She waved an arm around the store. "Look around. Take your time. If you don't see something you're looking for, just ask."

Cam took Marissa on a tour of the place. "I was thinking we should buy a single tail," he said, noting with pleasure the dilation of Marissa's pupils and the small shiver of excitement that moved through her as she stared at the array of whips hung artfully along one wall. "We'll pick one out today, and then there's one more thing I want to show you."

After Marissa had looked at everything she wanted to, and they'd agreed upon a small purple single tail for their purchase, Cam led her to the glass jewelry counter. "Today," he informed her, "we're getting a second ring." He had thought about how he would phrase it, as a question, or as a statement, and had decided on the latter. It was time to resume his role as Marissa's Master, and to trust her enough to know she would respond in kind.

"Oh," she said softly, bending over the glass to examine the jewelry displayed on black velvet shelves inside.

Cam pointed out a ring identical to the one he'd first picked out for Marissa prior to the piercing ceremony at Jack's place. "We'll take that one," he informed Celia. "Oh, and a spool of that pink satin ribbon."

Marissa turned a questioning face toward him. "What—" she began.

Cam smiled and placed his finger lightly over her lips. "You'll see," was all he said.

~*~

Marissa tingled with anticipatory excitement. Though she hadn't even realized it until now—she'd been waiting for Cam to come back to her. Or no, that wasn't precisely correct. She'd been waiting on a subconscious level for him to bring *her* back. Dana's talk with her couldn't have come at a better time, and she couldn't help but wonder if someone—maybe Jack?—had talked to Cam too. He was different, or rather, he was himself again.

On the subway ride back to Queens, Marissa had examined the second tiny gold ring perched so prettily in its blue velvet box. But what had really intrigued her was the small spool of pink satin ribbon. Cam refused to say what it was for, only that she would see. He did share that he was going to pierce her second labia when they got home. She was aware he'd pierced many slaves-in-training, and knew exactly what he was doing, but still the thought of the sharp needle piercing her delicate labia sent a shudder of delicious fear through her, as did his promise of what would come next.

"To celebrate your second piercing, we'll try out the new single tail. It's been too long since you were marked, slave girl."

She'd melted into a puddle of lust at his declaration, the words out of her mouth before she realized she was going to speak. "Thank you, Sir. Thank you."

Now she climbed into the shower and soaped her body before reaching for the razor. She stroked her mons with the blades so she would be perfectly smooth for the piercing. Drying herself quickly, she came into the bedroom. Cam was lying naked on the bed like a Greek god, his large, thick cock casually fisted in his hand as he read a magazine. He looked over at her, a sensual smile on his handsome face.

"You will go to the dungeon to wait for me," he said in a deep, sexy voice. "You will wear your collar and your wrist and ankle cuffs. You will wait in a kneeling, forehead press position until I come for you. Is there anything you want to say before you go?"

"I love you, Sir."

Cam's radiant smile warmed her from the inside out. "And I love you, sub girl."

In the dungeon, Marissa buckled her thick black leather collar around her throat, and welcomed the mantle of submissive serenity that settled itself over her senses. It was the strangest feeling, one she was hard-pressed to put into the proper words. Just beneath a deep and abiding sense of peace lay a simmering excitement, like water in the seconds before it rolls to a boil.

She retrieved her leather cuffs and clips, and wrapped the soft leather bands around her wrists and ankles, using the O rings on each to clip the cuffs closed. She positioned herself on her knees on the carpet square in the center of the dungeon. She leaned slowly forward until her forehead was resting on the floor, her arms stretched out on either side of her head, and waited.

It wasn't long before she heard the dungeon door open. She didn't move. She heard Cam enter the room, his bare feet sliding over the smooth hardwood until she felt his presence in front of her. His hand moved slowly over her bare back, his touch sending a shiver of pleasure to her core. He tapped her shoulder, and she rose as gracefully as she could, keeping her eyes submissively downcast.

Cam held the new whip, along with the velvet jewelry box and the spool of satin ribbon. He moved toward the small end table beside the spanking bench and set down the items. Returning to her, he took her face into his hands and kissed her mouth with a possessive growl as she melted against him. He took a step back, his hair falling sexily into his eyes, which were staring hungrily at her.

"Are you ready for my second ring, slave girl?" he asked softly.

"Yes, Sir," Marissa moaned. Her clit was already throbbing, and she knew she was sopping wet with anticipation. Cam led her to the spanking bench. She sat on the edge and he pressed her gently down onto her back on the padded leather.

"Scoot your ass to the edge of the bench, and keep your feet flat on the floor on either side," he instructed. "You will not move from that position until I'm done."

As Marissa adjusted her body on the bench, Cam stepped out of her vision. She could hear him rummaging in the supply cabinet at the back of the room. He returned a moment later with his piercing kit, which he set on the end table.

She couldn't stop the tremor of lust that shivered through her when he gripped her left outer labia between thumb and forefinger, and gently cleaned the area with a sterile pad. He selected a needle and pulled it from its protective plastic sheath, holding it so Marissa could see. "This piercing has no less import than the first, my darling. Even though there's no one else to witness this ceremony today, I will ask you again—are you ready to take my needle, and to wear my ring as a symbol of my ownership and possession of your heart, body and soul?"

"Yes, Sir," Marissa whispered, her heart beating like a small drum in her chest. "Please, Sir."

The needle was sharp, and she felt the burning sensation as she had the first time, and then the ring was in place, and it was done. As before, a rush of pure joy hurtled through her body, along with a fierce sense of pride and empowerment.

She lifted herself to her elbows to see Cam kneeling between her knees, his eyes bright with a blend of lust and adoration that nearly took her breath away. "You're ravishingly beautiful," he said, his voice husky with emotion.

He reached for the spool of satin ribbon. "Do you know what this is for, slave girl?"

Marissa suddenly realized its intended use, but she wanted Cam to say it, and so she said only, "Tell me, Sir."

"When you're properly healed, I will lace this ribbon between the rings and tie it into a little bow at your cunt." He reached out and touched the tip of his finger to her swollen, aching clit. "Only I will be allowed to untie the ribbon, when I decide to allow you to pee, or when I want to fuck you, or to whip your hot, sweet cunt."

Marissa could only moan in response.

Cam stood and with an evil grin, extended his hand to her. "But that will have to wait a few days. Meanwhile, I want to christen your new whip. Since your sweet cunt needs to heal, I'll be using that pert little ass of yours after you're properly marked. I assume you have no problem with that?"

"No, Sir," Marissa answered fervently and with complete sincerity. "No problem at all."

Chapter 13

BDSM equipment had been cleared on one side of the inner room, and a special dining table had been set up with a snowy white linen tablecloth, china and crystal, on which a sumptuous meal had just been served and consumed. Jack, Tony and Cam sat on chairs spaced around the table. Jesse, Dana and Marissa knelt on silk cushions beside their respective Masters. Two members of The Power Exchange waitstaff moved quietly around the table, unobtrusively clearing away the dishes. Jack had enlisted Stella, in her black leather apron, gold hoops dangling from her large nipples, and Steven, in his black leather vest and matching pants, to serve the meal, which Jack had had specially catered for the evening.

The club wouldn't be opening for another hour and a half, giving them ample time for the after-dinner ceremony the three Doms had planned. Cam looked down at Marissa, his heart surging with happiness. Though he'd always wanted someone to love, he had actually convinced himself over the years that being a BDSM trainer was nearly as fulfilling as having his own slave girl to cherish. What he hadn't realized was that love didn't just enhance a D/s connection—it transformed it.

Marissa must have felt his eyes upon her, because she looked up at that moment, her face breaking into a radiant smile. Her back was straight, her lovely breasts thrust proudly forward. She was wearing a sheer white dress that did little to hide her naked body beneath it. Her expression was serene, her hands resting easily on her thighs. Gone was any trace of nervousness or trepidation. She seemed completely at peace and happy in her role as his sub girl. And tonight, he hoped, they would take the next step.

Jack lightly tapped his crystal wine glass with a spoon, and all eyes turned to him. "Thank you all for joining me this evening. I know I speak for Tony and Cam when I say how deeply honored and proud we are to have such devoted and loving submissive partners." He looked down fondly at Jesse. "To honor our subs, we've agreed each of you should go up to the dais in turn to allow your Master to demonstrate your submissive poise while undergoing an exercise of our choice."

Jack pushed back his chair and stood, nodding to Jesse. "Jesse and I will start. We've been working on some bondage techniques we'd like to show you." Jack picked up a long duffel bag he'd placed on the floor before the meal, and together the two men ascended the set of portable stairs beside the small stage.

Jesse was wearing his usual outfit of a pair of loose white linen pants, his feet bare, the green leather and gold slave collar around his neck. Jack placed the duffel on the stage while Jesse untied and let his pants fall to the ground. He stepped out of them and crossed his arms behind his back. Jack stood beside him, a small single tail whip in one hand, a coil of thin, red rope in the other.

"Who do you belong to?" Jack asked Jesse in his gravelly voice.

"You, Sir," Jesse replied.

"What do you want me to do to you?"

"Whatever pleases you, Sir."

"It pleases me to bind you and mark you."

"Yes, Sir. Thank you, Sir."

During this exchange, Jesse's cock rose as if being inflated by a tire pump. As it extended to full erection, Cam could see jewelry from his piercing glinting on the underside of Jesse's cock. Jack touched the handle of the whip to Jesse's lips, which instantly parted. Jack placed the whip handle between Jesse's teeth, which clamped down on it.

Moving behind him, Jack bound the sub's arms, working quickly. When he was done, he tapped Jesse's shoulder, and the younger man pivoted gracefully so his back was facing the group. Jack, a Shibari expert, had executed a series of beautiful knots that bound Jesse's arms in a box position with what looked like a butterfly made of rope inside the box. Another tap had Jesse turn frontward again, the whip still caught between his teeth.

Jack took the whip from Jesse's mouth. Reaching into his pocket, Jack pulled out a long, thin strip of supple leather, dyed the same rich green as Jesse's collar. He looped and knotted one end through the ring of Jesse's cock jewelry. Pulling the leather strip upward, he touched the other end to Jesse's lips. Jesse opened his mouth and then closed it again on the leather, biting down.

"While I whip you, you will keep the leather in your mouth," Jack informed his sub, who nodded.

Jack took a step back. The whip whistled and struck Jesse's smooth, white chest, leaving a red stripe in its wake. He struck the man's thighs, leaving even, parallel lines along each leg. He tapped Jesse's shoulder, and Jesse turned, again showing the beautiful knot work along his back. His hands were clenched into fists, the only sign of any stress.

Jack wielded the whip with expert finesse, painting welts along Jesse's shoulders and drawing a crosshatch pattern over each firmly-muscled ass cheek. He tapped Jesse again, and when Jesse turned this time, Cam could see the sheen of sweat on his face, and the heave of his chest, but through it all, Jesse hadn't made a sound, and the leather strip remained clenched in his teeth, pulling his cock tautly upward.

"Are you ready for the final strike, slave boy?" Jack growled.

Jesse nodded.

As the whip struck his cock and kissed his balls, Jesse's eyes fluttered shut and he swayed a moment, as if he might fall. Jack dropped the whip and gently took the leather from Jesse's mouth, replacing it with his lips. Jesse opened his eyes as Jack stepped back, and even from his vantage point several feet away, Cam could see the love light in Jesse's adoring expression.

Jack bent to unloop the leather strap from Jesse's cock jewelry. "You may thank me," Jack said with a wolfish smile.

Jesse lowered himself to his knees and leaned forward to fervently kiss the tops of Jack's black boots. After a few moments of this slavish devotion, Jack tapped his lover's shoulder once more. Jesse stood, and Jack moved behind him, quickly untying the ropes that bound his arms. Jack turned to the group and smiled, his eyes glowing with pride. "Thank you all for witnessing my slave's grace."

With a nod from Jack, Jesse descended the stairs and walked back to his cushion at the table. Jack remained on the stage. Cam could feel Marissa tense suddenly beside him. Catching her eye, he shook his head. *Not yet*, he mouthed, and she relaxed.

Tony pushed back his chair and stood. He looked down at his wife and held out his hand. "You ready, darling?"

"Always, Sir," Dana said with her usual impish grin.

They walked to the dais and moved up the stairs. Jack stepped back to give them room. Tony removed his shoes and set them on the edge of the stage. Dana, who wore a clingy black dress that revealed as much as it covered, slipped the straps from her shoulders and shimmied sexily out of her clothing, though she kept on her shiny black heels. The diamonds on her nipple rings glimmered in the light. Her body was long and lean, and while Cam admired her athletic beauty and easy grace, in his mind it couldn't hold a candle to Marissa's feminine curves and skin soft as satin. He glanced down at his darling. She was watching the stage, her lips softly parted. *Soon*, Cam thought, *you'll have your turn.*

Tony addressed the room. "Dana has been working on focus, and we'd like to demonstrate that tonight." As he spoke, he unzipped the fly of his black trousers and stepped out of them. Dana knelt in front of him and reached for his underwear, which she pulled down his legs, revealing a semi-erect cock. Meanwhile Jack had retrieved a long, thin cane from his duffel. He stood just behind Dana, cane in hand.

Dana rose on her long, coltish legs. Tony put his hands on his hips and gave her an imperious nod. Dana bent forward at the waist, seeking Tony's rapidly rising cock with her mouth. She cupped his balls in one hand and gripped the base of his shaft with the other as she closed her lips lovingly over him.

Tony gave Jack a nod, and the cane came whooshing down against Dana's bare ass. Marissa sucked in her breath beside Cam. Dana flinched as the cane struck her, but otherwise didn't miss a beat. Jack struck her again, and again her muscles tensed, but her focus remained where it should be—on her Master's cock.

It took twenty strokes before Tony finally let out a groan and thrust his hips forward as he grabbed Dana's head to hold her in place. Jack lowered the cane and moved toward the stairs, which he descended quickly, his part of the ceremony completed.

When Tony let Dana's head go, she knelt back on her heels, her eyes fixed on his cock. Tony retrieved his underwear and pants and pulled them back on. Then he reached for Dana with both hands, pulling her up into his arms. He kissed her mouth lightly and murmured something in her ear. When he let her go, she turned so her back was to the room, and they all saw the dark welts that crisscrossed both ass cheeks like slashes of red paint.

"Oh," Marissa gasped softly, but when Dana turned back to face them, her eyes were shining, a beatific smile gracing her features.

Cam touched Marissa's shoulder, his heartbeat quickening. "It's our turn," he said softly.

~*~

Marissa took Cam's offered hand and let him pull her to her feet. Though she hadn't had any of the wine that had been served with the meal, she felt dizzy with nervous anticipation. While she had come a long way on her submissive journey, she had no idea how she would measure up to the stunning grace both Jesse and Dana had exhibited up on the stage.

She was now comfortable with public nudity, and confident in her ability to submit to Cam when they scened both in the outer room and in the privacy of their home, yet the thought of standing on the raised dais, the sole focus of all attention in the room, made her heart quicken and her mouth go dry.

At the same time, she was ready, and determined to do as well as the other two subs had done. Cam believed in her and, more importantly, she believed in herself. He hadn't told her just exactly what he had planned for her, but Marissa found she didn't need to know. It was enough that he wanted her to submit. It was enough to know she belonged to him—heart, body and soul.

They climbed together to the stage. Cam took Marissa's hand and together they faced their friends. "Marissa has been working on trust, as well as focus. She is learning to shut out all outside stimuli, and give her complete attention and submission to the task at hand." He turned and smiled at her, giving a small nod that was her cue.

Marissa slipped the straps of her dress over her shoulders and let it fall from her body. The pink satin ribbon between her legs was soaked with her juices from the excitement of the evening. Cam often tied it in place in the mornings before she left for work, a small but powerful reminder of his ownership throughout the workday. He had made even the act of using the toilet an erotic event, as she had to seek him out in order to get permission to pee. While she knew those who didn't understand the lifestyle might be appalled by the restriction, she had to admit it thrilled her to her bones.

"Lie down on the stage," Cam said to her now. "We're going to suspend you upside down for this particular exercise."

Whatever she had expected, it hadn't been that! Cam had suspended her in their dungeon, but never upside down. The prospect excited her, as she loved the feeling of erotic helplessness being suspended engendered in her. Being upside down would only make it that much more intense.

She lay obediently on the stage. Cam wrapped a large leather belt around her waist. It had built-in wrist cuffs on either side, and he placed her wrists securely in each cuff. Next he wrapped thick, sheepskin-lined cuffs around her ankles and clipped them to long chains that had been waiting in a neat row at the back of the stage. Tony handed him up a small stepladder, which Cam opened by Marissa's feet. Taking the lengths of chain, he climbed the small ladder and secured them to sturdy hooks that protruded from a winch apparatus in the ceiling. Climbing down from the stepladder, he closed it and set it aside.

Crouching beside Marissa, he kissed her lightly on the lips. "Ready, sweetheart?" he asked softly.

Marissa nodded. "Yes, Sir." Her heart was beating in a slow, steady rhythm and she felt unexpectedly calm.

Cam slipped his hands supportively beneath her as Jack pressed the button on the wall unit that activated the winch. Marissa's legs were slowly lifted as the chains wound around the winch wheel. Cam supported her as her body was hoisted into the air, until only her hair was brushing the floor of the stage.

Leaning between her still closed legs, he plucked at the pink satin bow and eased it from her labia rings. She heard the whir of the winch engine as the chains were separated, causing her legs to spread wide.

"I'm going to blindfold and gag you, and put plugs in your ears," Cam said in a voice designed to carry. "Your sole focus should be on my touch. You have advance permission to come. We will show our friends that my slave girl withholds nothing from her Master. You will give of yourself as you have never done before."

"Yes, Sir," Marissa managed, the calm of a moment before slipping a little, though her resolve had not.

Cam slipped a cloth gag between her teeth and tied it behind her head. He tied a second sash over her eyes and then pushed earplugs gently into her ears. The soft sound of her heartbeat was like listening to a seashell, and in the darkness and the silence, she found herself relaxing once more. She knew if she panicked for any reason, she had only to flex her hands into fists, but she also knew she had nothing to fear with her Master. She trusted him completely. She trusted him not only with her body and her heart, but with her very life.

It was impossible to tense in her position, but she liked to think she would have remained relaxed no matter the circumstance as Cam pressed a lubricated anal plug into her ass. She had come to enjoy the full feel of the plug, especially during intercourse, and she welcomed it now. She waited in the silent stillness for whatever would come next.

His fingers startled her at first, their touch light as feathers moving over her already swollen clit and labia. He slipped a finger inside her and drew out the moisture, gliding his fingers in an intensely pleasurably swirl of sensation over her cunt. He was standing close to her, and she could smell his masculine, woodsy scent and feel the press of his hard body against her side. He pushed two fingers deep inside her, and she groaned against the gag, a shudder of raw pleasure spasming through her frame.

As her Master rubbed and fingered her, she swayed gently in the dark, sensual silence of her chained and suspended captivity. It wasn't long before the orgasm sparked like a fire in her belly, and her entire body trembled as a long moan of pure lust rose in her throat. She began to thrash as the orgasm continued to pummel her senses.

It was perfect, perfect, perfect, and then... *Oh god, too much, oh stop, oh please, oh yes, don't stop, not ever. I want to die like this. I will die like this. Oh god, oh Sir, oh Cam, save me, take me, claim me, I am yours, yours, yours...*

She was sliding down a long tunnel into the perfect darkness, which enfolded her into its velvet arms as she slid peacefully away.

Marissa blinked against the light. She was lying on the stage and the chains had been removed. It took a moment to orient herself, and then she saw Cam's handsome face looming over her, and it all flooded back like sunlight.

Cam smiled. "There are you. We lost you for a minute there. Where did you go?"

Marissa sat up slowly. She was at once energized and deeply serene. She felt, in a word, amazing. "Where did I go?" she echoed, unable to wipe away the goofy grin that slid onto her face. "I went to heaven. You took me there."

Cam gathered her into his arms and pulled her to her feet. Someone had placed a stool nearby, and Cam helped her gently onto it. Marissa looked out toward the room, surprised to find it was empty.

"Hey," she said, confused. "Where did everybody go?"

"They went to the outer room. I told them I needed a moment alone with you. We'll join them in a minute."

Marissa frowned, a pinprick of worry stabbing through her serenity. "Is everything okay, Sir? Did I do something wrong?"

"No, oh no, not at all. You were spectacular. I was as proud as I've ever been."

"Then…?"

"There's something I wanted to ask you in private." He faced her with an earnest expression. "Marissa, here in the inner room is where we truly found each other. I know how scary it was for you — to take the initial leap of faith. You trusted me enough to be vulnerable and exposed about secret desires you'd always kept close to your heart. You were strong and brave, just like you are in every aspect of your life. You found the courage to move forward, even when some really tough stuff happened." His face darkened a moment, and Marissa knew he was thinking of Phil Mitchell. But he shook away the thought with a toss of his head, and Marissa was glad.

Cam took her hand, his voice softening. "There's something you need to know. You didn't just learn what it is to submit with grace and courage. You taught *me*, Marissa, what it is to trust my heart to another human being. Each step of the way, you were my shining example of what love can truly be."

To her astonishment, Cam knelt in front of the stool. Reaching into his pocket, he took out a small box. "Marissa, you are not only my sub girl, but my best friend. I love you with all my heart, and I want you always in my life."

He opened the box, revealing a diamond ring nestled in the satin. He looked up at her, his brilliant blue eyes shining hopefully. "Sweetest Marissa, will you marry me?"

Marissa felt her heart swell with such love it actually ached. Tears filled her eyes, while at the same time joyous laughter bubbled from her lips. "Oh, Cam!" She held out her hands, and Cam took them, rising to his feet.

Marissa stood and wrapped her arms around her Master, her partner, her best friend. "Yes, my love. I will."

Available at Romance Unbound Publishing

(http://romanceunbound.com)

A Lover's Call
Accidental Slave
Binding Discoveries
Cast a Lover's Spell
Caught: Punished by Her Boss
Claiming Kelsey
Closely Held Secrets
Club de Sade
Confessions of a Submissive
Dare to Dominate
Dream Master
Face of Submission
Forced Submission
Frog
Golden Angel
Heart of Submission
Jewel Thief
Julie's Submission
Lara's Submission
Obsession: Girl Abducted
Pleasure Planet
Princess
Sarah's Awakening
Seduction of Colette
Slave Academy
Slave Castle

Slave Gamble
Slave Girl
Slave Island
Slave Jade
Sold into Slavery
Submission in Paradise
The Auction
The Compound
The Contract
The Inner Room
The Master
The Story of Owen
The Toy
Tough Boy
Tracy in Chains
True Kin Vampire Tales:
    Sacred Circle
    Outcast
    Sacred Blood
True Submission

Connect with Claire

Website: http://clairethompson.net
Romance Unbound Publishing: http://romanceunbound.com
Twitter: http://twitter.com/CThompsonAuthor
Facebook: http://www.facebook.com/ClaireThompsonauthor
Blog: http://clairethompsonauthor.blogspot.com

CPSIA information can be obtained at www.ICGtesting.com
Printed in the USA
LVOW05s0113291014

410993LV00020B/1777/P